The Corn Marigold
and other Hebridean stories

Peter Marshall

Colinsburgh Press
2018

For Marion
Who took me to the islands.

By the same author
The Children of Kali

CONTENTS

The Corn Marigold
and other Hebridean stories

The Button

The water was cold. A late summer chill was in the air as Catherine Maclean dragged the wet kelp up the stony beach and dropped it above the tide line. The sun was just above the western horizon. She needed to get back, there was a meal to cook. The cut kelp would dry in the wind and the rain would wash it clean of salt. She started to fill her creel with the brittle dried kelp she had cut a week ago. The cry of the shearwaters made her look up towards Hallival. Their cries on the wind heightened the silence of the bay. As a child, before the Great Leaving, the foreshore would have been full of songs, laughter and chatter as the women and old men harvested great piles of kelp for the lazy beds. But this was a distant memory now. For years she had cut the kelp alone.

At the time of the Great Leaving Catherine's father, Alan, alone of all the islanders, had been allowed to stay. Catherine remembered holding her mother's hand by the small quay as friends and relatives, her whole human world, were forced onto boats. The tears and the cries of loss and anger had upset her and she hid her face in her mother's apron. Her mother made her wave goodbye to her grandparents and cousins. It had started to rain. Her mother called it God's tears at the injustice. A dog, abandoned for want of space in the boats, had swum after its master. Catherine had seen its bloated body washed up on the stones a week later.

Lachlan Maclean's men had torched the thatch of the empty houses. A pall of smoke had hung over the island as the black houses burned. When the rain had put out the fires and the wind had cleared the air a silence had fallen over the land.

New men came with their families and with them came the sheep, but the voice of the island had changed. The newcomers had been forced from their homes on Skye and the mainland and they brought their bitterness with them. The trust of the old days was gone. But it all came to nothing for the devil and whiskey did for Lachlan Maclean's grand plans.

Catherine had been too young to realise what her staying meant. She was eight when her brother Kenneth was born. It had been a difficult birth, and within the year Catherine's mother had died. The domestic chores and the raising of her infant brother fell to her alone. Before she was a woman she was burdened with the cares of motherhood. When she was eighteen she had been courted by Neil MacKay, a fisherman from Eigg. He had seen her on the shore and had asked after her. He visited her and she liked him. He had dark curly hair and laughing eyes, and he didn't drink. For a year he persisted but Catherine's father wouldn't allow it, for he was a Catholic and Catherine had responsibilities; Kenneth was only seven and her father needed her. She refused Neil and his disappointment turned to silent anger. She had seen him in Kinloch two years later. She had heard that he had married a girl from Skye. She thought to greet him but he turned his eyes from hers.

Catherine lifted the creel up and swung it onto her back. It would have been good to have bairns of her own and to see her future in their smiling faces, but the gift of motherhood had been ignored for too long. There would be no bairns now.

She made her way along the shore of Loch Scresort. A party of women was making its way to the pier from the grand White House, a departing house party, guests of the island's new owner, Lord Salisbury. Catherine sat on a boulder with her head turned while they passed. It was not from deference or embarrassment; it was a way of blocking them out. But she couldn't block out their harsh and insistent voices, cackling like geese in their foreign tongue. They were a strange people, selfish and demanding. They seemed only concerned with themselves, unaware of anything other than their own world and desires. Catherine knew she was invisible to them.

The women passed by. Servants followed them with trunks and cases to load onto the boat waiting to take the party to Mallaig. The men followed their women to the pier; superior and dominant, they frightened Catherine a little. They were accompanied by two sour faced ghillies, harsh men answerable only to Lord Salisbury, a distinction that excused them from common decency towards their fellow islanders.

The party was boarding the boat as Catherine crossed the gravel path on her way home. It caught the light and glinted. Balancing the weight on her back she bent down slowly and picked it up. It was a button, fancy and expensive, made of porcelain with a red rose painted on it. She thought it vulgar and brash, the colours unnaturally bright. Her first instinct was to return it to its owner, but the women would resent the intrusion to their giggling and effusive farewells on the pier. She would give it to Flora Macinnes' girl, Maggie. Maggie would like its brightness and could wear it as a brooch, or a medallion.

Her father Allan was sitting outside the cottage. He was old and his illness had left him weak and forgetful. Catherine slipped the weight of the creel off her shoulders and rested it by the cottage wall. She helped her father into the cottage and as she made bannocks she told him of her day and the party leaving the island. She placed the button on the windowsill so she wouldn't forget it.

Kenneth was due back. He had been working on the Kinloch burn, helping build some kind of dam for Lord Salisbury. The men had stayed in tents for five days. On the third day Catherine had taken her brother some broth and bannocks and decided to walk on to Kilmory Bay. She hadn't been there since a child. Then she would go regularly with her mother who would visit her sister. Catherine remembered playing with her cousins on the white strand. It had been a place of people and flowers. She had liked the way that the black houses nestled close to each other behind the rocky bluff, protection against the Atlantic storms. The narrow main street that snaked its way through the settlement was a place of gossip and meeting, a warm place for a child, dominated by a solid matriarchy of caring hands and watchful eyes.

All that was left were the moss-covered outlines of the buildings, the stone mostly taken for walls and sheilings. The flowers had gone, cropped by the sheep. Their inane call was the only company in a place grown desolate. Catherine hadn't tarried there. She had left and made her way home. It was not a thing to dwell upon, there was too much to do.

Catherine built up the fire. Her father was dozing. She peeled the potatoes and gutted the fresh mackerel. Kenneth would be home soon. He was a fine man and she knew that Jean Mackay was sweet on him. The thought troubled her but that was selfish so she put it out of mind.

She sat by the fire as the potatoes boiled and waited in the silence of the cottage for Kenneth to arrive.

The Corn Marigold

It was his daughter Anne's enquiry about her doll's house that led the Reverend David Wishart to climb the stairs of the manse with his two excited granddaughters in tow.

'The one that grandfather made for me. You didn't throw it out did you? I'm sure Lucy and Emma would love to play with it.'

Of course he hadn't. It was in the box room at the top of the stairs.

Emma ran up the stairs and stopped at the locked door. She rattled the handle.

'Come on, Grandpa.'

'Patience, Emma...'

David Wishart stopped on the landing.

'...is a virtue.'

He took the key from his waistcoat pocket.

'Can I open the door please?'

Lucy had mounted the stairs behind David and, aged ten, had the composure to win over her grandfather, a skill that Emma, six years younger, had no need of and so had yet to master.

David gave the key to Lucy.

The room was full of objects that had lost their immediate utility or relevance but for reasons of sentiment or future potential could not be thrown out. Cases, pictures and furniture competed with books, crockery and worn carpets for space. David hadn't been in the room for several years and he was tempted to open an old wooden trunk that had belonged to his father to remind himself what was stored there. However he moved it to one side and, as he suspected, the doll's house was lying behind it.

'Here we are girls.'

David pulled the doll's house upright and moved the trunk to allow Lucy and Emma space.

'Your mother's grandfather built it for her when she was your age.'

Lucy looked in through the windows of the house.

'It's lovely, Grandpa.'

She swung the front open.

'There's no furniture.'

David looked in.

'Ahh, yes.' He paused. 'I think we put them in a box in the trunk.'

David opened the trunk. On the top was a portfolio of paintings and next to it a paint box. The portfolio caused him to stop, as if it had caught him off guard. As he lifted it from the trunk some paintings fell out. Lucy picked one up. It was of a simple yellow flower painted in detail with delicacy and care.

''It's a flower, Grandpa.'

'Yes, a corn marigold.'

'Did you paint it?'

'Yes. It was a hobby of mine when I was a young man.'

'It's very good. Do you still paint?'

Before he could answer David noticed that Emma had found the box of paints and was tasting the watercolours. Her lips and chin were scarlet and her fingers threatened to streak her white pinafore. With a handkerchief and spittle he managed to wipe off the worst.

'Who is this?'

Lucy was holding a sketch of a young woman sitting on a rock and looking into the distance.

David took the sketch from her.

'A girl I knew. A long time ago.'

'Was she your friend?'

'No, not really. She showed me where some flowers were. I don't even remember her name.'

David looked away. The lie hurt him but he could not bear to say her name. It was foolish, over forty years had passed, a whole lifetime, but the guilt still disarmed him.

He remembered leaving The Glebe. Charlotte Morrison had arranged for Andrew to take him to Castlebay but without the courtesy of a farewell.

~ ~ ~ ~ ~ ~ ~ ~

Painting the flowers of the Western Isles to create a record for future generations of the glory of the Lord's creation had seemed so worthwhile. He remembered sitting with Euphemia in her father's house in Edinburgh, on his lap an edition of Linneaus's *Flora of the British Isles*. On the page plants were organised by kingdom, genus and phylum, their Latin names giving solid classical credence to the taxonomy. Each entry was illustrated by a drawing which had been painted, somewhat crudely David felt, with a wash that gave a thin approximation to the natural colour of the plant.

'Oh, Effy, look at this.'

Euphemia Chalmers, sitting in her parents' drawing room, had been watching David for some forty minutes. She had busied herself with sewing but was impatient to enjoy the delights of the well-tended garden and the warm autumn sun outside.

Euphemia put down her sewing and standing behind David's chair glanced at the open book.

'See *glebionis segetum*. It's from the Holy Land originally.'

The coloured drawing was of little interest to Euphemia who put a hand on David's shoulder and squeezed it lightly in an attempt to break the hold the little flower seemed to have over her fiancé.

'It's very interesting, dear.'

'Apparently you find it all over the Western Isles. Incredible that a plant our Lord Jesus looked upon can now be found on the edge of Europe.'

Euphemia took the book from David, ostensibly to get a closer look.

'I am sure that you could do better than that.'

She indicated the drawing without relinquishing the book.

'Oh, look, Father has returned from the Assembly with Reverend Morrison. Let us join them.'

Euphemia closed the book and returned it to the shelf. David gazed out of the window. Alec Chalmers and Reverend Morrison were inspecting Mr. Chalmer's roses.

The two men turned and watched David and Euphemia as they made their way down the terrace and onto the lawn.

'David.'

Alec Chalmers held out a hand.

'I'm so glad you could make it. Let me introduce
Reverend Morrison. He's the Minister for the Island of
Barra. Arthur, David is being put forward for the Parish
of Auldearn. He's been an Elder at St Cuthbert's these
last three years.'

Arthur Morrison smiled as he shook David's hand.

'It's a good living. I didn't know that Reverend MacLeod
was retiring.'

Alec laughed. 'He's being encouraged to go. He must be
seventy five if he's a day'.

'Well, Mr. Wishart, if you get the living we will share the
same landlord.'

'Of course. Colonel Gordon. I hear he's an improving
landlord.'

'Stern but fair. Stern but fair.'

The repetition brought the subject to a close.

Euphemia took her father's arm and they walked down
the garden admiring the roses.

'Barra, Sir. That must be a challenging living.'

Arthur Morrison shook his head in resignation.

'I won't pretend it's easy. The peasantry is primitive and
ignorant and, I'm afraid, have fallen victim to the
superstitions of the Catholic Church. They are indolent
and fatalistic and dwell in terrible poverty. They prefer
starvation to industry. It is very sad. Thankfully the
Colonel has encouraged independent farmers of

Presbyterian stock to settle on the Island. It not only increases my congregation but improves the land as well.'

They caught up with Mr. Chalmers and Euphemia, who was smelling a rose.

'Reverend Morrison was telling me about Barra.'

Euphemia smiled.

'I think you must be very brave to live there. It is so remote. Your poor wife must want for sophisticated company, yourself excepted of course.'

'You cannot deny a calling. There is much work to do there.'

'Well, I won't let David drag me so far from Edinburgh. I don't think I could bear it.'

Alec Chalmers plucked a rose and gave it to his daughter.

'You must stay for dinner, David.'

'Thank you, Sir. I will.'

'Now, if you will excuse us, Reverend Morrison and I have some matters to discuss.'

David watched as the two older men made their way solemnly back to the house and Euphemia, smelling the rose, watched David.

'I was being serious, David. Promise me that when we are married you will not drag me to some wild and remote island out of a sense of duty.'

'Auldearn is not like Barra. It is very close to Nairn.'

Euphemia made a face.

'Yes. Full of red faced farmers and surly fishermen. A parish here in Edinburgh would suit me well. I will even allow you Portobello.'

David chuckled. 'I'll have a word with the Moderator. Do you fancy a walk before dinner?'

Euphemia took David's arm.

In the drawing room after dinner the women sewed while David, Reverend Morrison and Alec Chalmers chatted. Reverend Morrison was short, well-built and, David guessed, in his late thirties. He had an infectious enthusiasm and talked at length of the plans to improve Barra.

'I rent a farm and we are improving the land. It's hard work but good work.'

He was certain in his views and concerning his plans he did not entertain the slightest hesitancy or doubt. The conversation turned to the changes in Edinburgh since Reverend Morrison's last visit.

'The stations down by the North Bridge are magnificent.'

Alec, in expansive mood, gestured with his right hand as if the station buildings were there in front of him. Smiling, Morrison nodded in approval.

Alec continued, 'Ahh, David, you didn't see it before. I remember I was at University when they finally filled in the loch. I would wander down to Princes Street from the New Town and watch the engineering works.'

'I hear that the loch was foul and pestilential.'

Alec chuckled.

'The stink was awful, David. It was a health hazard. Cholera, typhoid, even malaria. The city fathers had no option.'

Alec warmed to his theme.

'Aye, it was for the Royal visit. They made The Prince's Gardens. That was a grand occasion.'

He smiled at David.

'Before you were born of course.'

He paused in reverie considering the transformation.

'Look at it now. A monument to progress, to human endeavour. When I was born the idea of an iron railway with steam locomotives was as fanciful as going to the moon. When my grandfather took a coach to Glasgow it took him a day and a half.'

Alec jabbed his finger towards David to emphasise his point.

'Today he could leave in the morning and be in Glasgow for lunch.'

Morrison agreed.

'Aye, Alec, you are right. It shows what the entrepreneurial spirit and capital can achieve. And it was a Scotsman, Adam Smith, who showed the way, and now we are seeing what can be done with industry and courage.'

'Exactly, Arthur. Exactly.'

Alec turned to David.

'Industry and commerce – the great engines of progress and change. And the secret is liberty, the freedom from preference or restraint and from interfering government. Let commercial society follow its own course. You can see the benefits all around us, factories, exports. The creation of wealth on an unprecedented scale.'

Alec was quite animated now but his enthusiasm had disrupted his chain of thought. He turned to Morrison.

'Refinement and liberty, wasn't it?'

Morrison calmly recalled the quote.

'Commerce and liberty, liberty and refinement, refinement and the progress of the human spirit.'

Alec beamed.

'Exactly. That's where to put your money David, in railways. The turnpikes?'

He laughed.

'Slow and unreliable. Even with the new tar roads, they are finished. Eighty miles an hour. Eighty. Think of that.'

Alec breathed in and shook his head in wonderment.

'A train going at eighty miles an hour. It's been done. Think of it – Edinburgh to Glasgow in less than an hour. Invest in the railways, that's my advice. It's the future.'

The wonder of the railways was exhausted but Alec was reluctant to let the expansive mood die. He smiled at David and shook his head.

'I envy you, David. Oh, to be young again! The modern world is exciting. There is nothing we can't achieve if we have the will and courage. Industry and capital – that's the answer. Industry and capital.'

David noticed Morrison nodding in agreement and heard him say quietly, 'And the faith Alec. Don't forget the faith.'

'I hear that you are interested in Botany, David?'

Reverend Morrison's enquiry caught David unawares.

'Yes.'

David cleared his throat.

'Yes. I thought of studying science before I took up Law. I am interested in the distribution of wildflowers, and the impact of habitat on their dispersal. Domestic flowers, like Mr. Chalmers' wonderful roses, are the result of man's cultivation, but wild flowers.'

David stopped. There was something about Reverend Morrison that made David feel he needed to be precise.

'It's...'

He paused again.

'It's how and why they end up where they are. Just today I was reading about *glebionus segetum*, the corn marigold. It is said to come from the Holy Land. Christ could have gazed upon it, but it can also be found in your part of the world, the Western Isles. Was it always there? How did it get there? The Holy Land and the Western Isles couldn't be more different.'

Morrison smiled.

'It doesn't surprise me. We may not have forests and rich farmlands on the isles but wildflowers we have, corn marigolds, bluebells, wild pansies and orchids.'

He raised his hands palms upwards to emphasise the wonder.

'Orchids in abundance. The dunes in early summer are a profusion of wild flowers. Botanists come from Glasgow University to study them.'

David didn't like the idea of professors from Glasgow getting there first.

'I would like to make a study of the wild flowers of the Western Isles. An illustrated guide.'

Alec chipped in.

'You should go. Visit. Arthur would put you up, wouldn't you, Arthur?'

David suddenly felt awkward. Reverend Morrison could hardly refuse, but really the invitation should have come from him.

'One day I would certainly like to see the islands and pay a visit to you, but I wouldn't dream of imposing on you. Anyhow, at the moment it is out of the question. I am far too busy at work.'

'David, it would be a pleasure to have you come and visit us. I know my wife Charlotte would be delighted to have a visitor from Edinburgh.'

The conversation lulled and Mrs. Chalmers looked up from her sewing.

'Euphemia, dear, why don't you play us something on the piano? I am sure Reverend Morrison would love to hear you play.'

Putting her sewing away, Euphemia walked to the piano. David felt proud as he watched her. She was a handsome woman, like her mother. Her dark blue velvet dress complemented her pale complexion and dark hair. She sorted through the music lying on the top of the piano and selected a sheet. She turned to the expectant audience.

'*Will Ye No' Come Back Again.*'

And her delicate fingers embraced the keys of the piano.

~ ~ ~ ~ ~ ~ ~ ~

David stood on the deck leaning over the rail watching the island of Rum passing on his right. The hills rose magnificently from the sea, their tops caught in cloud. The air was clear and the island seemed close. It looked forbidding, treeless and desolate, with no sign of habitation. The boat gently shook to the reassuring throb of the engines and he looked back to the flock of gulls following in its wake. In two hours the ferry would be docking at Castlebay. The Reverend Morrison had written saying a cart would be waiting at the pier. David walked across the deck and took a seat on one of the benches. He shared the bench with a woman in a bonnet with her arms around a large basket that rested on her knees. Next to her was a young lad dressed in grey woollen trousers and a dark blue jersey. The boy stared at David with an alarmed interest. Just as David was about to reassure the lad with a friendly greeting the woman barked at her charge in Gaelic and as the boy looked away the woman returned to her privacy, gazing at the horizon ahead.

The day was warm and, with the August sun on his face, a mood of well-being settled on David. He watched as the distant hills of Skye passed by and was glad to be out of Edinburgh. He wondered if the prospect of a break had intensified his mood, but he had begun to find life in the capital tiresome. The legal work in Mr. Chalmer's chambers did not excite him and although he loved Euphemia dearly the constraints of Edinburgh society had become predictable and tedious and he longed for a living away from the city. The prospect of a whole month on Barra and South Uist, walking and painting in a wild and unfamiliar landscape, excited him. In March a letter had arrived from the Reverend Morrison inviting David to stay for the month of August. He had apologised for the delay in writing. He had been busy with work on the estate and domestically the house had been in upheaval due to the birth of Mabel, the latest addition to the family.

'However affairs are on an even-keel at present and I very much look forward to sharing with you the plans we have for the island.'

David remembered Reverend Morrison talking with great enthusiasm about the modernisation of the island; the resettlement of the land in an economic and sustainable manner and the introduction of profitable economies that would lead to the development of drainage schemes, roads, schools and much else. It would be grand to see these improvements at first hand. David noticed that the boy was staring at him once more. He had a worried mien; his skin was sallow and his face drawn. He didn't respond to David's smile, so David got up and strolled to the bow of the ferry to watch its progress towards the outer isles which had come into view.

As David waited on the jetty at Castlebay for his trunk to be landed from the ferry he looked across to Kisimul Castle standing forlorn and abandoned on an island in the bay. It seemed to rise straight out of the sea. He had read that it had been emblematic of the power of the Macneil Clan. But their rule was finished and he could see it was too modest to be of interest to the new laird, Colonel Gordon.

Bags of flour, crates of groceries and barrels were being unloaded by a group of local men. The voices and laughter of the men disrupted, yet emphasised, the quiet of the harbour; so unlike Greenock from where he had embarked two days ago. David had felt lost and overwhelmed in the noise and industry of the port, a continual clamour of steam and metal, a cacophony that was only escaped as the ferry steamed its way down the Clyde.

The unloading finished, a pile of crates waited on the jetty to be picked up while others disappeared with the men on drays and carts. Once they had departed the quiet was only disturbed by the gulls and the distant throb of the ferry as it made its way out of the bay.

David looked up towards the town. Castlebay barely imposed itself upon the landscape; the houses were scattered across the hill that gently rose from the bay. The settlement looked half-finished, as if it was waiting for the rest of the residents to turn up. A group of women was chatting by some lobster creels. Their conversation didn't miss a beat as they turned to look at the stranger. David smiled and raised his hat, a courtesy the women's gaze ignored.

'Mr. Wishart.'

David turned. A man was walking down to the harbour. Behind him was a boy pushing a wheelbarrow.

'I'm Duncan MacFarland. The Reverend Morrison sent me to bring you to The Glebe.'

The man was soft-spoken, tall and bearded. David's trunk was placed in the wheelbarrow and the three of them made their way to a waiting horse and cart. Duncan lifted the trunk on to the cart and the boy jumped up after it. Duncan mounted the cart and slowly filled a pipe without venturing any conversation. Once the pipe was lit he twitched the reins and the cart started on its ponderous way.

They soon left the scant settlement of Castlebay, slowly travelling north on a gravel road. On the left the cart passed by a loch in the middle of which was a small ruin sited on an island. On the opposite side of the road David noticed a collection of dark, thatched buildings. He thought that they might be barns but noticed smoke rising from them, and that old folk were seated outside. Children stood impassively watching the cart make its way while a couple of dogs ran down to the track barking.

He wanted to ask about the ruin and the paupers' cottages but Andrew was a man of few words and the boy, seated on the trunk, was preoccupied by the view of the track from the back of the cart.

As they came over a rise David noticed a larger township of wretched dark buildings set back on the right, cowering in the lee of a stony hill. In contrast, on David's left, the white beaches and sand dunes of the machair came into view. The late afternoon sun made the white sand shine and the light glistened off the foam-tipped waves as they washed the beach. For an hour they plodded north as the sun lengthened in the west. Their slow progress suited David; he was in no hurry and was enchanted by the landscape, with its outcrops of grey rock pushing into the sea and the sand dunes speckled with wildflowers. He noticed groups of people busy on the distant beach. He asked Duncan what they were doing.

'Collecting shellfish.'

The reply was given without Duncan's eyes leaving the track and David let the matter lie.

Eventually they turned east and as the road made its way between two low hills David saw The Glebe and beyond it the solid, modest building of the 'new' Kirk. Grey-slated, harled and standing at three storeys, the Glebe was an impressive house, bigger than any David had noticed in Castlebay. It was protected from the winds by a grey stone crag that rose to the north. It had a neat garden at the front and was flanked by fields of sheep. The cart pulled into the yard behind the house where David was met by a tall woman. Holding her hand was a small girl who watched David as he climbed down from the cart.

'Mr. Wishart, I'm Charlotte Morrison. Welcome to the Glebe.'

David shook the outstretched hand.

'A pleasure to meet you, Mrs. Morrison.'

'I hope your journey was trouble free.'

'Thank you. The sea was mercifully calm.'

The young girl was pulling at her mother's arm.

'Ah, yes, this is Victoria. She has been beside herself with excitement all day in anticipation of your arrival.'

David held out a hand.

'I'm very pleased to meet you, Victoria.'

Victoria suddenly became shy and, clinging to her mother's arm, turned her head away.

'Duncan, put Mr. Wishart's trunk in the hall. Arthur sends his apologies. He's been organising the mending of some fences, to keep the sheep off the cliffs. It's a never-ending problem. You must be weary. I'll get Mary to make us some tea.'

Another servant, Emma, showed David to his room. A welcome bowl of hot water was waiting for him and after washing away the grime of the journey he joined Mrs. Morrison and Victoria for tea. Victoria had overcome her shyness and plied David with questions about Edinburgh, its castle, the railways and other topics decided on at random until her mother sent her to her room to get ready for her dinner.

'You must excuse her, Mr. Wishart, The prospect of a visitor from Edinburgh has had her excited for days.'

It was early evening when Arthur Morrison returned home. He radiated the energy of a working man as he vigorously shook David's hand.

'Mr. Wishart, so good to see you. I hope the journey went well.'

Without waiting for an answer he spread his palms out and looked at his shirt.

'Look at me. I'm filthy. I need to wash. I'll see you at dinner.'

The dinner was most welcome. Food on the journey had been variable. The roast leg of lamb surrounded by roast potatoes looked more than inviting. Arthur started carving the meat.

'Our own lamb, raised on the machair. I can guarantee it will taste excellent.'

As they ate Arthur talked about his plans for the farm, which seemed to coincide with the future of the island.

'This lamb,' Arthur held up a piece speared on the tines of his fork, 'would find a ready market on the mainland. With the new steamships and railways, Glasgow and Edinburgh are within reach. And not only lamb. We raise excellent beef as well.'

As the lamb eventually found its way into Arthur's mouth Charlotte took the chance of the enforced pause to address David.

'Arthur tells me that you are a painter and are interested in the flowers of Barra.'

'Yes. I hope to make a record of the variety of species to be found on the island, especially on the machair.'

'Well, you will certainly have a lot to interest you. Victoria was very excited when she heard that you painted. You must not let her annoy you. She can be very insistent.'

And so the evening went on. Good food and pleasant company, the conversation invigorated by the optimism and enthusiasm of Arthur and Charlotte. As David knelt by his bed to give thanks to the Lord and ask forgiveness for his sins he felt a contentment in this wild beautiful place that he could not have imagined in Edinburgh.

Maybe it was the excitement of a new place, possibly the novel morning sounds of sheep and chickens, or the brightness of the Hebridean light, but David rose early. Susan MacNeil, a plain shy young woman, was raking the fire while Emma brought in pails of water to heat for the Morrison's morning wash. Emma smiled nervously at David and wished him good morning.

'Would you like some tea, Sir?'

David declined and establishing that breakfast would be at 7.30 he decided on a walk. With no sense of urgency he strolled north and then turned west over dunes towards the sea. The new light was crystal and the early morning breeze sharpened his senses. He climbed a low outcrop of stone and from the top had a fine view of the sea and the coast stretching for several miles south. The magnificent white beach and the sand dunes covered with marram grass caught his eye, yet it was the ocean that captured his imagination. The breeze was light but the sea, enraged by some storm far out in the Atlantic, burst upon the shore angry and vengeful. Vast and unknowable, it dominated his view. In comparison the coast looked fragile and the island small and vulnerable. The sound of the surf and the call of the gulls filled the air, making David feel more alive than he could ever remember. He looked north towards the outlying islands and the coast of South Uist stretching away in the clear morning sunlight.

David decided to make his way down to the beach and walk back to The Glebe following a burn that ran into the sea. He crossed the burn where it met the beach and scrambling up a high dune could see the roof of The Glebe about half a mile away. Heading towards the road that had taken him to The Glebe the previous day, he saw smoke rising from a cottage. He was surprised that he hadn't noticed the cottage before. It was one of those ramshackle affairs that seemed to litter the island. He decided to take a closer look, and as he approached he saw three women watching him. One of the women was seated, her face was lined and she looked as old as time itself. The other two women were much younger but any traces of youth were masked by their careworn and drawn faces. Their clothes were patched and filthy, the old woman's shawl stained and threadbare. The cottage looked primeval. Built of stones, mud and thatch, it gave the impression of having grown out of the land. It had one small window and a door that would disgrace a potting shed. David greeted them but they ignored him. One of the young women went into the gloom of the cottage. The other two women watched him in silence as he made his way to the road.

'We have been improving the grass in these two fields, clearing rocks and weeds and spreading seaweed.'

David and Reverend Morrison were standing on a low grassy knoll with a good view of the fields leading down to the sea.

'We don't have to worry too much about drainage here. The machair is very sandy. It's important to keep it well manured though.'

He smiled at David.

'Good grass means good livestock.'

He pointed across the road to rough ground rising towards some hills.

'When we expand over there it won't be so easy. It is very boggy and will need a lot of drainage.'

'You have grand plans, Arthur.'

The intimacy of last night had put them on first name terms.

'Aye. This is a great island but it needs organisation and hard work. It's been neglected for too long.'

He stood surveying the landscape, momentarily lost in a vision of how things could be.

'Come. I must show you my church.'

They walked across the machair towards the road and for the second time that day David found himself approaching the ramshackle old cottage. The old woman was still sitting by the door. She was knitting and watched them approach. One of the young women, digging seaweed into a small plot of land to the side of the cottage, stopped briefly and glanced at the two men before returning to her task. Arthur Morrison stopped. David thought that he was going to greet the old woman, who must be one of his parishioners, but instead he turned to David.

'This is the problem, David, ignorance, poverty and fecklessness. These people have been struggling, scraping a meagre living out of this land for generations. But now there are too many of them and in their ignorance they refuse to change. The world has moved on but, caught in a world of superstition and idleness, they can't see it. A few years ago on this very island they were dying in their scores from dysentery and cholera. They have no idea of basic sanitation.'

He pointed at the old woman who met the privilege of being singled out with a stony stare.

'Her husband died. Of cholera. You would have thought that would have shown her the need for change. But, no. These people can't imagine anything other than the miserable lives they lead. It's sad.'

Arthur Morrison shrugged his shoulders, turned and made his way to the road.

'You will have noticed on your drive up here how many of these blackhouses there are and it's worse on the east of the island. Each one of them crammed with impoverished souls living in squalor.'

Arthur Morrison stopped and looked back at the blackhouse.

'Like animals.'

He shook his head in despair.

'And, you know, the real tragedy is that we get reports from the colonies, from Canada and America where islanders who have emigrated are doing well. They own acres of land and employ servants and labourers.'

He gestured to the blackhouse.

'But they won't leave. We even offer them free passage to Canada but they won't go.'

He climbed over a style onto the road. David followed him.

'You say that you offer them free passage but still they won't go?'

'Yes that's about the sum of it.'

'Why?'

'I blame the Catholic Church. They control this island. They have a strong hold over the islanders, who, on the whole, are simple and superstitious. I believe that a lot of them come from Irish stock. It is in the priest's interest to keep them ignorant and beholden. We do our best. When the potato crop failed we organised road building and drainage schemes in return for food, but there is only so much you can do. A Catholic cottar doesn't have the same work ethic as his Protestant neighbour.'

Arthur Morrison had reached the church. He stopped with his hand resting on the church gate.

'They have a church at Craigston. They call it the mother church with its incense and popish idolatry. The peasantry here is dominated by the Catholicism of the bog Irish. My church is spartan in comparison, but there is a strength in that, as I know you will agree, David. And it's a good congregation and growing.'

They entered the church. In the east wall were four windows looking onto a rough field and a stony outcrop, yet the west wall was windowless. Arthur gestured towards the windows.

'The glory of the God of Israel was coming from the east.'

He laughed.

'The truth, I am afraid, David, is less prosaic. As the congregation grows we will be able to develop the church on the west side. The cost of windows was deemed an extravagance.'

Arthur Morrison looked around the small room.

'We keep it plain and simple here.'

He smiled and rested his hand on David's shoulder.

'We save our efforts for prayer and hard work. Come let us pray.'

They knelt facing the altar.

'Dear Lord, please bless our efforts to improve this place and build a congregation of true believers. Give us the strength to toil ceaselessly and not shirk the difficulties that confront us. Help us to choose the right path and not be tempted to take the easy way. Make our ministry strong and pure. Amen.'

For the next few days the weather set fair allowing David the luxury of exploring the island. Arthur Morrison had told him that the west coast lying to the south of the Glebe was the best for machair, and although the summer was well advanced the wild flowers were still abundant. Each morning, before the Morrisons had breakfasted, David set out with his leather shoulder-bag packed with his sketch pad, notebook and a lunch of bread and cheese prepared by the Morrison's cook, Mary Fraser. He soon found a spot with a remarkable variety of marsh orchids and lost himself for hours sketching and recording those he recognised. He decided that he needed a technique for recording his findings, so he chose an orchid and counted how many there were in a twenty foot square. He wasn't sure if this was scientific but he was certain that the information would be useful. He then set to sketching the flower from various angles, before filling in the colour. This was the most difficult part. David had been a competent draughtsman since his schooldays at George Heriot's but mixing an exact colour from his palette of watercolours was time-consuming, yet essential if his record was to be accurate. Occasionally his patience became strained and after several hours of careful sketching and painting he allowed himself the abandonment of a landscape watercolour. The landscape excited him, the magnificent light and the ever changing sky contrasting with the silent solidity of the hills. He loved the way that the colour of the sea deepened farther out from the shore and he tried to capture its different moods. And as he painted he could hear the wind, the cries of the gulls and the murmuring surf.

On the third day, after several hours of careful attention to a clump of purple and blue self-heal, he decided to walk along the beach to stretch his legs and ease his cramped joints. He noticed three women collecting seaweed. Two of them were the women from the blackhouse by the road, and with them was a much younger woman with long raven hair. She was no more than fifteen, barefoot and thin. She wore the air of despondency that seemed to settle on the islanders. They were gathering seaweed and putting it into large creels.
He raised his hat and greeted them. They stopped and stared at David for a while as if unsure as what to do. Then one of the woman spoke to the other two in Gaelic

and they resumed work. David retired to a rock on the shore and while they worked he made sketches of them. As he drew he imagined a large oil painting of the wild Hebridean landscape and the peasants in honest toil on the shore. He allowed himself the delightful fantasy of having it accepted by the Royal Academy at their summer show. While he sketched the women hoisted the full creels on their backs, the young girl, despite her youth, having equal share of the burden.

He watched them as they trudged up the beach and eventually disappeared into the sand dunes. It pained him that he couldn't speak with them. There were so many questions that he would have liked to ask.

When David returned that evening, Arthur was in his study preparing a funeral service. Charlotte organised tea and scones and asked David if he would do sketches of Victoria and the infant Mabel. The likeness of Mabel asleep in her mother's arms was easy to capture and David insisted that the portrait be completed in watercolour. Victoria, however, was too excited to stay still long enough for anything but a quick sketch. Victoria was convinced that David shared all her enthusiasms. David enjoyed the childish meanderings of her curiosity but Charlotte, with maternal firmness, kept in check her daughter's attempts at monopolising David's time.

Sketching finished, Victoria produced her copy of *Aesop's Fables* that she was certain David had never read but would enjoy. As they sat on the sofa she selected a fable and read it with remarkable confidence for a girl of her age. She had been taken by the fable of the *'Town Mouse and the Country Mouse'*.

'You see, Mr. Wishart, you are the town mouse and I am the country mouse. But I don't think I would be scared in Edinburgh. Do you? '

David paused for a minute, giving the idea due consideration.

'I don't think so. I live in a very nice part of Edinburgh. And anyhow my fiancée Euphemia and I would make sure that you would be very safe.'

Victoria thought long and hard over this and her conclusion was only articulated by a sigh and a nod of the head. She randomly turned the pages until the title of another fable caught her interest.

"The Two Frogs", she announced. She looked at David. 'Do you like frogs, Mr. Wishart?'

'I like them in ponds and in my garden because they eat up the slugs that ruin my flowers.'

Victoria read the story out loud of the two frogs, one living in a deep pond far removed from public view and the other in a miserable gully close to a road. The more fortunate frog entreated his friend to join him in his pond which was safer.

'*The other refused, saying that he felt it so very hard to remove from a place to which he had become accustomed'.*

Victoria stopped.

'That's like the people who live in those dirty cottages. Father says that they would be much better off going somewhere where they can make a living. What do you think, Mr. Wishart?'

'I am certain that your father is right, Victoria. But it is difficult to leave somewhere that you love.'

Victoria returned to the fable.

'*A few days afterwards a heavy wagon passed through the gully and crushed him to death under its wheels.*'

She looked up from the book and held David's eyes with her own while reciting the moral of the fable.

'*A wilful man will have his way to his own hurt.*'

Charlotte placed the sleeping Mabel in her crib and turned to Victoria.

'Time for bed, Miss Morrison.'

David had been staying with the Morrisons for ten days when the pleasant evening routine was disrupted by a guest for dinner.

'Mr. Wishart, let me introduce my good friend, James Balfour.'

They shook hands.

Balfour was a tall, dour-looking man who didn't grace Arthur's introduction with a smile.

'Mr. Balfour lives in Eoligarry House, the finest house on the island. And this April I had the decided privilege of conducting Mr. Balfour's marriage to Miss McKenna.'

David smiled.

'May I offer you my congratulations.'

Balfour nodded. He was obviously a man of few words and with the absence of his new wife David got the impression that his visit was more to do with business than a social call. The meal was subdued. Mr. Balfour showed no interest in David or his reason for visiting, although at Arthur's prompting he mentioned that an ornithologist had been staying at Eoligarry House.

'It would seem that the flora and fauna of the Hebrides are of considerable interest to the outside world. Would that there was an equal interest in the economic problems afflicting these islands.'

'Yes. Arthur has explained the problems you have with excess population and starvation.'

Balfour put down his knife and fork and sipped from his glass of wine. David caught a shadow of concern darken Arthur's face.

'Mr. Wishart, you have probably read in *The Scotsman* and *The Edinburgh Weekly Chronicle* letters from the like of Donald McLeod on how we mistreat the noble highlanders of these islands. How we starve them and strip them of their dignity. What you won't read is how we provide them with work, of how Colonel Gordon has invested many thousands of pounds in this island and how, despite all our efforts, the cottars and crofters, these noble clansmen, can't even organise themselves to pay their rent. On average each croft is six months in arrears. Some are a full year behind and with no means of making up the deficit. I can't see a city landlord being so lenient with his tenants in the tenements in Edinburgh or Glasgow, can you?'

David felt he had unwittingly become party to a conspiracy against the tacksmen of Barra and was wondering how he could protest his innocence without furthering Mr Balfour's ire when Arthur came to his rescue.

'I think that you will find, James, that Mr. Wishart is aware of the efforts of Colonel Gordon to improve his estates. He is soon to be adopted for a living in the Parish of Auldearn on the Colonel's estate near Nairn.'

This information returned Balfour to his previous taciturn mood. Charlotte took the opportunity to chat lightly with David about Euphemia until the meal was finished and Arthur and Mr Balfour made their excuses and went to Arthur's study. As Susan cleared away the plates Charlotte apologised.

'You must forgive James his brusque manner. He has a very large estate on the island and also one on South

Uist. He works very hard and has so many problems with his tenants. Life at the moment is not easy for him. Affairs on the island, as you will be aware, have been very difficult in the last few years, especially with the potato blight. He does his best and feels he gets no support, only criticism. I know he didn't mean anything personally.'

When David was invited by Arthur to accompany him to observe the sheep shearing on Balfour's estate he assumed that it was Arthur's way of mending fences.

'We have hired some men from Skye. We can call upon the local population but, frankly, they are not good workers and seem to bear some resentment towards James, and, if I am to be honest, towards myself as well. You see, they tend to blame us for their own misfortunes, but their circumstances, if truth be told, are due to ignorance and a refusal to change with the times. It is, of course, convenient and reassuring to have a scapegoat. Either way that does not concern you, David, and it is great sport watching the men bring the sheep down from the hills with their dogs. The men from Skye are exceptionally skilled.'

The clouds were threatening rain and so they donned their coats. Arthur lent David a walking stick with a handle carved from a ram's horn.

'You look quite the shepherd, dear chap. The shearing is great fun. You can even try your hand at it if you like.'

A group of dozen men with dogs were gathered around a cart. James Balfour was in earnest conversation with two of them when Arthur and David arrived. Arthur joined James but David held back although he was pleased to get a nod of recognition from Balfour. The group set off up the hills accompanied by a cacophony of whistles and calls. The dogs, which up to then had been docile, even listless, sprang into life and tore up the steep sides of the hill to bring down the sheep scattered randomly over a vast area. David accompanied Arthur, and although he was certain that each man was carefully engaged in a sophisticated strategy that would outwit the nervous and uncooperative nature of the sheep, the overall plan was obscured by what seemed to him men and dogs striding off at random in different directions. Arthur was with one of the Skye men, tall and rangy with a full beard. He commanded a couple of lean dogs that watched his every move. Arthur spent his time in conversation with the man and David, not wishing to interrupt, was content to spectate.

After hours of distant cries and whistles echoing around the hills David observed what, for him, seemed like a miracle. Groups of sheep, huddled together for safety and severely policed by dogs, were making their way off the hill and were driven into a secure field. Soon David was deafened by the persistent, mournful bleating of sheep. The shearing had started before all the sheep were off the hills and David watched in awe as the Skye men roughly grabbed the sheep and turned them on their backs in one deft movement inducing an unlikely passivity in the otherwise nervous and excitable animals. The shearing, which seemed to David a delicate operation, was done with an insouciance and speed that betrayed a life of practice since a young age. Pleased that he had brought his drawing pad, David started sketching the men at work, who thankfully paid him no mind.

Afternoon was drifting into evening when David, who was sketching men rolling up the fleeces into bales and then piling them on the carts, became aware of an altercation. James Balfour was striding towards a man dressed in black who was standing at the edge of the field talking to some of the shepherds. Balfour was waving his stick and shouting at the man and although David couldn't make out what he was saying Balfour's anger was obvious. He was followed by Arthur and for a moment David was afraid that they would both attack the man. Balfour, however, stopped short and, with his stick raised, shouted abuse so close to the man's face that the spittle from his imprecations spattered his adversary. The man did not move or respond and for a moment there was a dangerous hiatus until Arthur restrained Balfour and the man turned and slowly walked away. The men fell back to work with a wary eye upon their employer while Arthur drew him aside and they fell into earnest conversation. Work continued as dusk fell.

It was late when David and Arthur walked back to the Glebe. Arthur was quiet and so it was David who brought the topic up.

'Who was the man who annoyed Mr. Balfour so?'

Arthur shook his head.

'He is an agitator. I wish James wouldn't get so angry. It plays into their hands.'

'An agitator?'

'He claims that he is a journalist but his first priority is not to report the news but to foment discord and unrest.'

They stopped by the church, its walls seeming to glow in the sunset.

'He is from Caithness, and most probably a member of the Free Church. We suspect that he is supplying the islanders with Gaelic Bibles and subversive literature also in their native tongue. He is against the landlords and gains a ready audience by blaming them for all the islanders' ills. If he carries on causing trouble we will have him in court. James is the magistrate so it should be an open and shut case.'

He turned for home.

'I would appreciate it if you didn't mention the incident to Charlotte. She tends to worry. Things haven't been easy since the potato blight.'
They continued to The Glebe in silence.

Although the shearing of the sheep continued the following day, Arthur had a funeral to conduct and David decided to return to his study of the wildflowers of the machair. He would forego the exotic charms of the orchids and paint *glebionis segetum*, the simple corn marigold that had drawn him to the island in the first place. To do this he ventured further south to the old burial ground. The machair was extensive there and Charlotte had told him that the flowers were abundant.
'The dunes are opposite the townships of Borve and Craigston. At Craigston there is a very fine sheep farm set up by Colonel Gordon. It shows what can be done with hard work and commitment.'

The machair, however, was a disappointment, being overrun by sheep brought off the hills and which were in the process of grazing the grassland to a short crop. So as not to waste the day David retraced his steps north to the beach he knew well and, as often happens when approaching a known location from an unfamiliar direction, the aspect became novel and he found a secluded dune partly hidden by a rock promontory. It was a tapestry of orchids, wild pansies, cotton grass and self-heal. The flowers grew profusely through and round each other, creating a glorious confusion of colour. With his back to an outcrop that stretched into the sea he began sketching and painting.

He plucked a wild pansy and placed it on a piece of white paper torn from his sketch pad. This allowed him to experiment by mixing his watercolours and daubing the paint next to the flower until he got an exact match. Next, he drew the flower on a blank background so that its features stood out. Painstakingly he painted each of the slim petals with delicate shading. David became absorbed by the task and only once he had finished did he become aware of how tense he had become bending over his painting board. Pleased with what he had done, he put the painting board down and stretched, easing the ache out of his back. It was then that he became aware of a young girl watching him. It was the girl he had seen gathering seaweed on the beach. He had no idea how long she had been there. She was sitting on a rock idly playing with her hair, dressed in the same worn, dun-coloured skirt and threadbare woollen shawl that she had worn before. She was looking at David with a curious intensity. He smiled at her and she looked away only for her gaze, which had a feral, inquisitive fear, to return from lowered eyes.

David grabbed his sketch pad and started to draw but the girl was suddenly distracted. The funeral procession with Arthur at its head was making its way along the road to the cemetery by the kirk. The girl got up and, crossing herself, ran to the road to watch it pass.

The meal at The Glebe that night was a subdued affair. Arthur had been distracted since the sheep shearing and the conversation at dinner rarely deviated from polite enquiry as to David's day. After dinner Arthur retired to his study to prepare Sunday's sermon. Charlotte, as genial as ever, was cryptic in her explanation.

'You must not mind Arthur, Mr. Wishart. He is very busy and pre-occupied at present; there are changes afoot.'

Victoria alone seemed unaffected by the mood and David spent the evening showing her the day's paintings over which she cast her critical eye and declared them 'Quite good.'

The following Sunday the Morrison household made its way along the three hundred yards to the church. Arthur Morrison, a dark coat over his surplice, was out in front, hurrying to greet his congregation. Behind him came Charlotte and then David. Victoria was holding David's hand, the young girl's act of ownership of the special visitor. Following were the servants, Mary Fraser, Emma Johnston, Susan MacNeil and Duncan MacFarland, all dressed in their dark Sunday best.

David was privileged to a seat in the Minister's family pew. Behind him was the small congregation, sturdy farming men and their families. They were listening to Reverend Morrison's eulogy to William MacIntosh, the member of the congregation whose funeral Arthur had conducted during the week.

'It was a long life and a good life. And we should all feel grateful that we knew him. When I had the honour to become your minister four years ago it was William MacIntosh who first welcomed me and my family.'

Arthur smiled towards William MacIntosh's sons seated to David's left. The eldest, now the head of the family, acknowledged Arthur's tribute to his father with a grave smile.

'He worked hard and he taught his three sons to do the same, for he saw in his industry not a means of self-advancement but a solemn duty to God our father. Today we know that he will be in the company of the Lord who will say *"Well done, thou good and faithful servant. Rest, for your work is done".* The Lord will reward every man according to his deeds, for does not Proverbs tell us, *"The way of the slothful man is as an hedge of thorns"*, yet it is also written there that *"To the righteous good shall be repayed"*. William MacIntosh was righteous and an example to us all. Would that many of our Island community had taken more heed of his exemplary life. There is a misconception abroad that some are born to poverty and destitution, that it is their natural lot, that they cannot help themselves. Such ideas are a blasphemy.'

Arthur Morrison paused to let the accusation take effect. When he resumed, his voice was soft.

'Is not the Lord God in his heaven the maker of all things? *"For God saw everything that He had made, and behold, it was very good"*. We are all put on this earth as stewards of God's wonderful creation. If through idleness the sluggard makes nothing of his time on this earth he is betraying the trust that God has put in him. All God's bounty here on Earth is given to us, not to take like a thief but to earn with hard work and in that work we show gratitude for God's love. The Bible is clear on this. Isaiah tells us, *"The Lord is a God of judgment; blessed are all they that wait for Him"*. And then in the Psalms we learn, *"He turneth rivers into desert, springs of water into thirsty ground; a fruitful land into barrenness, for the wickedness of them that dwell therein"*. There are those that say take pity on the poor, but is not the Lord the author of all things?'

Arthur's voice rose.

'Does the Lord take the innocents, the thrifty, the hardworking and cast them aside and leave them destitute?'

He raised his arms with his palms upward in theatrical disbelief.

'What blasphemy is this that suggests the Lord is vindictive and unjust? Saint Paul tells us in his Letter to the Romans that the Lord *"will render to every man according to his deeds"*. So those who will not work, who choose indolence and a love of superstition over obedience and hard work, should not be surprised if the Lord turns his back on them, for He says in Hosea, *"For the wickedness of their doings I will drive them out of mine house"*.

Reverend Morrison had warmed to his theme and his tone brooked no contradiction.

'Those that suffer starvation and destitution, and there are many on this island, should look into their hearts and not seek to blame others. Micah said of the wicked, *"The land shall be desolate because of them that dwell therein, for the fruit of their doings"*. I know for some of you this may seem harsh, but the time is coming when retribution will be demanded and given. That time cannot be stayed for ever. We must remember what happened to the Israelites when they turned away from God, for there are those amongst us for whom Babylon awaits. Let us pray.'

While David collected the Bibles and hymn books from the pews and took them to Victoria who stacked them in the cupboard in the vestry, Charlotte and Arthur chatted to parishioners outside the church. The sermon had worried him. There was too much Old Testament retribution and vengeance and nothing of the love of Christ.

Victoria checked the Bibles.

'Ninety seven , ninety eight, ninety nine, one hundred. Good. That's all the Bibles.'

'There were only thirty Bibles laid out. Why did you count them all?

Victoria looked at David with pity verging on contempt.

'That would be silly. You must count them all.'

She raised her finger.

'Never a slacker be.'

David wasn't sure that there was such a saying, but he let it pass.

Charlotte looked in.

'Come on, Victoria. Time to go.'

As Charlotte and Victoria walked back to The Glebe hand in hand Arthur came into the vestry and put on his coat. He seemed much cheerier than he had been of late.

'What did you think of the sermon, David?'

David paused.

'It was very powerful.'

'Yes, I felt so. The trouble is that we are preaching to the converted in this church. It is the congregation at St Brendan's in Craigston who should have been listening. Mind you, the Father at St Brendan's only deals in half-truths and Popish idolatry.'

He held the church door open for David.

'St Brendan's.' Smiling, Arthur shook his head in mock dis-belief as if savouring a private joke then, as he closed the door, he announced in faux solemnity, *"The Lord will not suffer the soul of the righteous to famish."* To The Glebe, Sir.'

Rain from the Atlantic washed out David's plans and it wasn't until the Wednesday of the following week that he returned to the secluded dune. The weather was dry but chill and, as she gave him a piece of mutton pie for his lunch, Mary Fraser had urged him to take a coat.

'There's rain on the wind.'

He had been painting for about an hour when he noticed a couple walking towards him along the strand. As they approached he recognised the young girl, who despite the cold wind was barefoot and wearing the same dark skirt and worn shawl. David suspected she had little else to wear. With her was the man to whom James Balfour had taken exception. They stopped and the girl pointed towards David. The man seemed to be questioning the girl before walking towards David with the girl a few steps behind. He was wearing the same dark suit and had the air of a man on a mission. He raised his hat in greeting.

'Good morning, Sir. I am Dugald Stewart. I am pleased to make your acquaintance.'

He held out his hand. David carefully put down his brush and got up.

'David Wishart, Mr. Stewart. How can I help you?'

'This is Eilidh.'

Dugald Stewart gestured towards the girl who would not meet David's eye but looked out to sea.

Dugald smiled.

'She told me of a strange man who seemed to be painting. She was curious as to what you were painting, and why?'

'I am not sure that I have to explain myself to this young woman.'

'I am sorry if I seem unfriendly, Mr. Wishart. Eilidh's enquiry is not in the way of an accusation. She walks this beach every day and I think for her curiosity to be aroused is not unreasonable.'

David wondered whose curiosity was being satisfied. He picked up his board. An unfinished painting of pink thrift was pinned to it.

'I am painting flowers. The flora of Barra.'

David offered it to Eilidh, who glanced at the board but made no attempt to accept it. Dugald took it and speaking softly in Gaelic handed the board to her.

'Eilidh does not speak English, Mr. Wishart.'

Eilidh looked at the painting closely and then looked at David before studying the picture further. She handed it back to David and muttered something to Dugald.

'She says it is very bonny. What brings you to Barra, Mr. Wishart?'

'I have come to paint the flowers, Mr. Stewart. The Western Isles have been neglected in most studies of the flora of the British Isles.'

'And you wish to remedy that.'

'I wish to make a record.'

Dugald turned to Eilidh and David assumed he was explaining David's purpose. He wished he could talk to the young girl directly.

'Eilidh says that she knows where there are beautiful flowers up on the hill yonder. She will take you there if you wish.'

'That would be kind.'

In truth David would have been happy to remain on the dune but the offer gave him the chance to question Dugald Stewart, whom he suspected might be able to shed light on the changes in Arthur Morrison's mood.

With Eilidh taking the lead the party made its way off the beach and on to the road that joined the Glebe to Castlebay.

'Are you from Barra, Mr. Stewart?'

'No. My father was a crofter in Sutherland.'

'But you are not a crofter?'

Dugald smiled.

'No, I benefitted from an education. My father was keen that I should better myself as he saw it.'

'And have you?'

'I am a man of letters and a journalist. If he was alive I think that my father would be proud of that. But I am proud to be his son. He worked the land with industry and honesty, was an elder of the Kirk and brought up four children to be God-fearing and respectful of their fellow man. I am not certain what more he could have achieved.'

They walked on in silence.

'So what brings you to Barra, Mr. Stewart?'

'Well it is not the flowers, Mr. Wishart, although I concede that they sing loud the glory of God's Dominion. It is his highest and most complex creation, man, that brings me to Barra. Or, to be precise, the depths to which he has fallen.'

'You talk of the poverty and indolence of the natives of the island.'

'No, Mr. Wishart. It is the fall from grace of the landlords and the men who do their bidding that interests me.'

Eilidh had run ahead along the road. She pointed in the direction of a hill and started up a rough track.

'This is where I leave you, Mr. Wishart. I look forward to our meeting again.'

With that Dugald raised his hat and made his way towards Castlebay.

The flowers that excited Eilidh were a bright yellow cluster of tansy along the bank of a stream, a common enough species and not what David was looking for. He could see how they impressed her but the location lacked the variety of the machair. Rather than disappoint her enthusiasm David smiled and set out his watercolours, pencils and his board. Fascinated, Eilidh watched David's preparations intently. He was about to start drawing but faint pangs of hunger reminded him of his walk up the hill. From his bag he took the piece of mutton pie that Mary Fraser had given him and broke it in two. He offered half, wrapped in paper, to Eilidh. She looked concerned but David thrust it towards her and she took it and gently put it into a pocket in her skirt.

After he had eaten David plucked a head of the small blooms and placing it on a piece of white paper started mixing his colours to find the right shade of yellow. Eilidh peered across at the preparations and David turned his board so that she could see what he was doing. Having mixed the paints David quickly sketched and started to fill in the colour. Eilidh's concentration waned and she started to gaze at the landscape below. Taking advantage of her distraction David took another sheet of paper and drew a quick sketch of Eilidh. She proved the perfect model as her attention to the view below kept her still. David caught her likeness and washed in some colour, which, although not detailed, gave the sketch a pleasing depth.

Just as he had finished Eilidh stood up and, pointing into the valley, said something in Gaelic to David. It was only after she had spoken that she realised that he did not understand. She put her hand to her mouth and smiled. David laughed. Eilidh shrugged and pointed into the valley. David held out the sketch to her. Tentatively she took it and gazed upon it in wonder. She offered it back to David who gestured that it was hers to keep. She smiled. He took a shilling from his pocket in payment for her time and because he knew she was poor. She looked at the bright shilling and her expression turned to one of alarm. Clutching her portrait, she ran off down the valley.

Mary Fraser had been right and the afternoon brought rain that saw David scuttling off the hill and back down to the Glebe. There was an afternoon somnolence about the house with the servants busy in the kitchen and Charlotte, Victoria and Mabel away visiting. David changed out of his wet clothes and reviewed the less than successful results of the day. He decided that the day could not be saved for meaningful endeavour and that he would retire to the library and read. It had a south facing aspect and there was usually a coal fire alight. When he entered the library he was surprised to find it occupied. Arthur Morrison, James Balfour and a visitor were seated round the fire in earnest conversation. The conversation stopped when David entered and Arthur stood up. He looked awkward, almost embarrassed.

'Ahh, David.'

He paused.

'We are rather busy at the moment, if you don't mind. Estate business.'

Arthur gestured towards the visitor.

'Mr. Ferguson has come from Cluny Castle.'

The visitor rose. He was tall and bearded, with a fine head of grey hair and wore an air of unquestioned authority.

'David, isn't it? How are you dear chap?'

He offered his hand and David took it.

'It's alright, Arthur, David and I are acquainted. I deal with Mr. Chalmers on legal matters for the Banffshire estates. How is Euphemia, David?'

'Very well thank you, Mr. Ferguson. At least, she seemed as much in her last letter.'

'Excellent. Now if you don't mind', Ferguson smiled, 'we are rather busy.'

The presence of Andrew Ferguson had surprised David. He had met Ferguson as Colonel Gordon's official representative in the Edinburgh chambers and twice David had been asked to prepare legal agreements for property bought and rented out on the Banffshire Estate. David had suspected that it was Andrew Ferguson's good reports about David Wishart that had opened the prospect of his receiving the living at Auldearn, reports in no little way coloured by David's engagement to Euphemia.

On Charlotte's return David learnt that Andrew Ferguson was staying at Eliogharry House with James Balfour. Over dinner that evening Arthur didn't mention Andrew Ferguson and so David had no idea of the reason for his visiting Barra. However, given the fact that Colonel Gordon's official representative was on the island, Arthur's reticence on his presence did nothing to assuage David's feelings of unease.

The next morning, David woke to a cool north easterly and the threat of rain and decided against painting. He needed to go to Castlebay and call in at the Post Office. He had a letter to send to Euphemia and he could collect the mail for The Glebe. The walk to Castlebay was refreshing with the sharp breeze on his back and the sea rushing in on the sands. He climbed the hill past Borve and gazed down on the scattered settlement circling the bay. As he entered Castlebay the air became filled with the smell of burning peat which he found more welcoming than the acrid sulphur of the Morrison's coal fire.

David posted his letter and collected the mail for The Glebe. As he left the Post Office he was greeted by Dugald Stewart.

'Mr. Wishart, how are you?'

'I am well, Mr. Stewart.'

David waited for Dugald to catch up with him. He was wary of the man but also felt that he might provide an explanation for the increasing unease David felt in the Morrison household, as if he had overstayed a once limitless welcome.

'Well met, Mr. Wishart. What brings you to Castlebay?'

'I came to post a letter and collect the mail.'

The answered was brushed aside as Dugald brandished a piece of paper in front of David.

'Have you seen this?'

'What?'

Dugald handed David the paper. It was a notice written in Gaelic with an English translation, calling the tenants of the Gordon estate to a meeting the following Saturday in Lochboisdale on the island of South Uist.

'No, I haven't.'

'The Reverend Morrison hasn't mentioned it to you at all?'

'No, but there is no reason he should. I am, after all, merely a guest painting flowers.'

Dugald Stewart's tendency to interrogate David annoyed him, but he held his temper. Dugald seemed lost in thought studying the notice.

'It has been handed out to all Colonel Gordon's tenants.'

'It is probably about rents.'

Dugald shook his head.

'No.'

He pointed to the notice.

'It says whole families are expected to go and if they don't they have to pay a two pound fine. See, it's signed by a Andrew Ferguson on behalf of Colonel Gordon. This Ferguson is staying up at Eliogarry House with Balfour. They know their tenants can't afford two pounds. They can hardly afford to feed themselves.'

'Well, I am afraid that I can't help you, Mr. Stewart.'

David turned to go.

Dugald Stewart seemed to relent.

'If you are walking back, Mr. Wishart, let me show you the east side of the island. I will show you Eilidh Macdougal's croft. She was very taken with the painting you gave her.'

David smiled.

'It was just a sketch. I offered her a shilling for her time but she wouldn't take it.'

They started walking out of Castlebay.

'She couldn't take it, Mr. Wishart. She wouldn't be able to explain the reason for your generosity to her father.'

David was appalled.

'You don't mean.... ?'

'Northing personal, Mr. Wishart, but it is common knowledge that Mr. Balfour has littered the island with his baseborn spawn.'

Dugald noted David's expression of disbelief.

'You find that hard to believe, Mr. Wishart. I am afraid that the position of tacksman puts power in the hands of many who have neither the moral compass nor the integrity to discharge their duties in a Christian manner. Balfour and his colleagues are driven by self-interest. If you are prepared to take a man's livelihood away to increase your landholding, taking his daughter for your own carnal pleasure is a minor transgression and can be marked up against rent owing, a debt that is designed never to be paid.'

'It is an easy and cowardly thing, Mr. Stewart, to slander a man behind his back, when he is not here to defend his honour.'

They had stopped in a bend in the road. Ignoring David's protest Dugald pointed towards a small township of five blackhouses situated on rocky uneven ground. They were wretched hovels and David found it hard to believe that people lived in them. They seemed more like mounds of stones and turf and only from one did smoke indicate habitation. From the door of another some ragged children were watching the two strangers with a dull curiosity that David had become used to.

'Now, why do you think that folk decide to live here? You can't cultivate the land and there's barely enough grass for a cow.'

'I am certain that you will tell me, Mr Stewart.'

'Well, it's not due to ignorance or indolence, as some would tell you. These families were moved here two years ago by Mr. Balfour and Reverend Morrison so that they could take over the land around Borve and The Glebe. Good land where you can raise cattle and grow your crops. And they moved these decent folk here, to nothing but rocks, and let them starve. That is fact, Mr. Wishart, not slander. The law may support their acts of persecution but I defy you to tell me that our Lord would admire such treatment of fellow man.'

They walked on with the sea on their right. David could see that the land was indeed poor and inhospitable. He felt uncomfortable. Should he believe this man so caught up in his own sense of self-righteous anger and thus betray Arthur and Charlotte Morrison, who had shown him such hospitality? Yet a doubt nagged at him, for how could men choose to live on such an inhospitable shore?

'Tell me, Mr. Stewart, what is your reason to be on Barra?'

'I thought I had told you that already, Mr. Wishart, but I will be more specific.'

Dugald Stewart stopped and sat on a rock that cut into the rough track.

'I have been told that Colonel Gordon wishes to clear this island of its surplus inhabitants. I cannot stop what Colonel Gordon wishes to do, but I intend to be here to record this act of brutality for posterity.'

'Given the way these people live, maybe it is for the best, Mr. Stewart?'

'To be taken against their will from the land of their ancestors and forced to be an immigrant in a land not of their choice? Tell me why they are so below the contempt of gentlemen such as Reverend Morrison and

Mr. Ferguson that no one asks them what they would like?'

'Maybe they are not in position to know what is best for them.'

Dugald Stewart looked at David long enough for his derisive snort to be calculated.

'Ha! So you, Reverend Morrison and Colonel Gordon know what is best for these people, whose families have lived on this land and scraped a living from its unforgiving soil for hundreds of years. Are you telling me that you know what they need better than they?'

'You seem an angry man, Mr. Stewart.'

Dugald resumed his progress along the track,

'Yes, you are right Mr. Wishart. I am an angry man.'

They continued up the track in silence for some minutes. They turned a corner where laid before them were a number of hovels crammed upon a small parcel of flat land. Dugald looked at David and then turned and looked at the blackhouses.

'My father was a crofter in Sutherland. He was called before the factor, a Mr. Sellar, to pay a sum of monies that it was claimed he owed. He had receipts and other vouchers proving payment and that should have been the end of it, except that the factor, like Mr. Balfour, was not only the factor but the Justice of the Peace as well. My father was called before the court and payment demanded. He refused as he had proof of payment but this was ignored. An estate commissioner, a Mr. James Loch, was brought up from London. My father had gathered signatures from the elders of the Church and the parishioners for a certificate of testimonial as to his honesty and peaceful character. Many hundreds signed but one did not – the Minister, Mr. Mackenzie. He regularly dined with the factor. Mr. Loch found my father guilty, a 'turbulent character' was how he described him for when my father asked that the Minister be made to swear on oath that my father was not an honest and peaceful character, Mr. Loch said that my father's actions accused the Minister of lying.'

'And was the Minister called?'

Dugald laughed.

'This was in November and the next night, a night of cold and driving rain, the factor arrived with eight of his men and they proceeded to evict my father from his house. All the furniture and his meagre belongings were thrown out and broken, and the family's bedding was thrown into the rain. I was at university in Glasgow at the time. I only wish that I could have been there. The factor threatened all the other cottars and crofters that if they gave my father and his family shelter then they would be evicted the next night. Every door was shut against my father and his family. They could find no shelter. My father caught a chill, and was dead within the week.'

'I am sorry to hear that, Mr. Stewart.'

'But that is not all. The factor took my family's croft for his sheep. Yes, I am angry, Mr. Wishart . My mother is a broken woman. What little money I earn goes to her and my two sisters, but I can never earn enough to ease my mother's pain.'

Dugald stopped and pointed to the settlement of blackhouses.

'This is Earsairidh ,where Eilidh lives. Come and meet her family.'

They walked up a track to the blackhouses. A woman met them at the door. She wore the usual dark woollen skirt with a shawl around her shoulders. Her face was lined and unsmiling and her hair grey. Dugald greeted her in Gaelic. She glanced at David and went inside.

'That's Eilidh's mother. Come.'

The interior of the house was dark and, although small, the far side was obscured by peat smoke. It took a while for David to get used to the dark but as he did he noticed an old man with white hair and beard seated by the hearth. Dugald greeted the man and they spoke for a while. David noticed the man chuckle when Dugald mentioned his name. With his eyes on David the man pointed to wooden chairs recently vacated by two young boys who watched the strangers through the smoky gloom. Dugald turned to David.

'This is Eoin Macdougal. He is the head of the family, and Eilidh's grandfather.'

David smiled and bowed his head in greeting. The man merely watched the gesture and spoke to Dugald.

'Eoin says he is pleased that you have honoured his house with your visit and offers you a cup of tea.'

'Oh, I don't think that is necessary.'

'It would be rude to refuse. Tea is only made for special guests.'

Dugald turned to Eoin and they chatted a while and David knew it was about him, for the old man's stern eyes rested on David. Unnerved by Eoin's interest, David looked around the blackhouse as a means of evading his gaze. The furniture was rude and plain; he imagined much of it was home made. There were few luxuries, a cheap print of the Madonna and Child in a frame and a gaily painted vase, home to a posy of wildflowers. The earthen walls had, in places, been lined by old newspapers, browning with age and the peat smoke. He noticed his painting pinned on the wall. David's gaze came to the door and he saw Eilidh standing in its light. With her was a younger girl; the family likeness suggested it was her sister.

'Mr. Wishart, Eoin wonders what you do for a living. You are a botanist, are you not, and a painter?'

Dugald's interest made David wary.

'I am a solicitor, Mr. Stewart. I work in Edinburgh. Botany is merely an interest.'

Dugald's brow creased.

'A solicitor? What is your speciality?'

'I deal with domestic concerns – wills, trusts, divorces, conveyancing. Nothing of much interest.'

David could see that this revelation disconcerted Dugald.

'However, I will soon be leaving the Law to become a Church of Scotland minister.'

He had hoped that this would reassure Dugald but all Dugald did was nod his head knowingly and turn back to talk to Eoin. David felt a hand on his shoulder and Eilidh's mother handed him a cup of tea and smiled to acknowledge David's thanks. In the smile David caught the likeness of her daughter and he could see that she was not as old as her careworn countenance suggested. The cup was of cheap china and had a chip out of the rim. David noticed that he was the only one given the precious tea and sipped it, forcing back concerns over hygiene.

'Eoin wants to thank you for the picture of his granddaughter. He says he will treasure it.'

David smiled and shrugged dismissively to indicate to Eoin that it was nothing, and for the first time since David entered the old man smiled.

It was obvious that Dugald had business to discuss with Eoin as they fell into a furious discussion in Gaelic, so once he had finished his tea David stood up and, thanking Eoin for his hospitality, took his leave. The weather was beginning to close in, with dark clouds banking up from the west. By his reckoning he had a further seven miles to The Glebe and hoping to evade the rain he set out at a brisk pace. A few yards up the track he turned and looked back at the sad collection of hovels. He saw Eilidh at the blackhouse door watching his departure. David waved farewell and was pleased when she returned his wave.

The rain had set in with a quiet persistence by the time David reached the Glebe. He gave the mail to Emma to take to Arthur and then he went up to his room to change while water was heated for a bath.

That evening Andrew Ferguson joined them for dinner and David was relieved to see that he was alone and to hear that James Balfour was in Lochboisdale. Arthur seemed much more relaxed and the dinner was very jolly, with Andrew Ferguson telling amusing anecdotes about the eccentric and reclusive Colonel Gordon.
'You know he has a map that marks all the toll roads in Britain and when he makes a journey he will go twenty or

thirty miles out of his way so as to avoid payment of a shilling. The man is worth millions of pounds. The other day, to avoid a toll of a few pence, he found himself on a rough track in the wilds of the Mearns and his coach broke an axle. He is a difficult man to comprehend and impossible to please.'

Despite the merriment and laughter David got the impression that the evening had a more serious purpose, one that involved him. When the meal had finished Charlotte excused herself and went to check on Mabel who had been suffering from gripe earlier in the evening. Arthur went for a bottle of port and on his return mentioned an urgent letter he had to write and get delivered before morning.

'I think that you will find the port is rather fine. I will be back shortly.'

Andrew Ferguson poured two glasses of port and, taking his seat opposite David, he slid a glass across the table.

'The Morrisons are a lovely people, but Arthur is not the most subtle of men. I asked him to leave us alone as I wanted to talk with you about the Auldearn living. You understand that to all intents and purposes it lies in my gift. The incumbent minister, the Reverend MacLeod, is, as you know, old and not in the best of health. He will retire very soon and the living will become vacant this autumn. I will be willing to promote your application for the living but before I do that I need to be sure that you understand what being a minister on one of Colonel Gordon's estates entails.'

Andrew Ferguson paused. David spoke.

'I have been an Elder at St Cuthbert's for two years, Mr. Ferguson, and have had the opportunity to watch Reverend Paul undertake his duties. I hope that you will agree that he is an estimable minister and thus an excellent teacher.'

Ferguson smiled.

'Indeed he is, indeed he is. It is not the discharging of pastoral care or the service that concerns me. On both these accounts I know that when called upon to undertake those responsibilities at St Cuthbert's you have been exemplary. A living on one of Colonel Gordon's estates has other responsibilities. You will be placed between the Colonel and his tenants, who will also be your congregation. Inevitably tension and possible conflict arises between a landlord and his tenants and when it does your parishioners may call upon you to intercede and take their side. In such an eventuality you must be perfectly clear in your own mind that your loyalty lies unwaveringly with Colonel Gordon. Since the Great Disruption you will be aware that the Highlands are full of self-styled Free Church ministers, the 'na daoine' as they call themselves. They spend more time preaching anti-landlordism than the gospels. They create dissent and seem determined to unleash the forces of anarchy on the world by destroying the very fabric of civilisation, which is respect for property. It is easy for those without responsibility to cause dissent. It is those with the responsibility of power, a terrible responsibility David, who take the difficult decisions and usually garner no thanks for their Herculean efforts.'

Andrew Ferguson sat back in his chair and took a sip of port. His words demanded no reply and David sat silent, feeling like a chastened schoolboy.

'You need to think deeply about this, David, and talk to Euphemia. To take up a living is not a decision to be taken lightly. To help you decide there is something that I would like you to do for me.'

'But of course.'

'As you probably know, we have a meeting in Loch Boisedale with the tenants on Colonel Gordon's estates in Barra and South Uist. I want you to come with Arthur and me and support us in what will be a difficult meeting.'

David was about to speak when Andrew stopped him with a raised hand.

'The matter is complex and I can't go into details now, but I would appreciate your support.'

The next day, Friday, David took his paints and brushes back to his favourite spot on the machair. His progress to the beach was watched by the women in the blackhouse with their usual silent hostility. He had realised that morning that he had yet to do a painting of a corn marigold, the plant that had first drawn him to the machair. He decided to do several sketches and paintings, for he had conceived the idea of a large canvas of crofters collecting seaweed, and in the foreground Eilidh, her creel by her side contemplating a corn marigold, the flower that Our Lord would have picked. He would call it *Blessed Are You Poor* and the message would be clear about the all-embracing love of Jesus Christ.

The weather was fine and the beach deserted. He had half-expected to see Eilidh collecting seaweed. He was, however, glad that he wouldn't be disturbed. He started work on single blooms. He loved the simple arrangement of petals and the uncomplicated bright and happy yellow that deepened in the central disk of its inflorescence. His first two paintings were executed in fine scientific detail, showing the composite nature of the flower, and then, to relax himself, he did a sketch in watercolours capturing, in broad strokes, its jolly exuberance. He then moved to clusters of flowers, with the yellow corn marigold jostling for attention with the purple and red of the self-heal, the white of the eyebright and the delicate blue of the harebells. After the rigour of the single blooms he found painting the energy and profusion of the machair flowers invigorating.

After several hours David stopped to eat the bread and cheese that Mary had prepared for him. While concentrating on painting he had managed to forget his concerns raised by the conversation with Andrew Ferguson, worries that had disturbed his sleep that night. It was clear that he was on trial; his loyalty was being tested and his future plans for a life with Euphemia could be dashed in the next twenty four hours. He was anxious about the meeting in Lochboisdale. He didn't like Dugald Stewart but could not suppress the thought that the journalist's claim that a clearance was being planned was probably correct.

He suddenly felt weary. He packed up his paints, put his paintings and sketches into his leather portfolio and, standing on the top of the dune, looked at the hills to the east. Turning his gaze to the machair and the sea rolling in along the white beach he felt sad, for he had a sense that his stay on Barra was coming to a close and this was the last time that he would be painting the flowers of the wild, magnificent landscape of which he had grown so fond.

On David's return The Glebe was full of piano music. Victoria was practising her scales and Charlotte was supervising her with Mabel on her lap. David went to the library and placed his day's work on the table. He was considering his first painting of the corn marigold when Emma Johnstone came in with a cup of tea. She glanced at the painting as she carefully placed the cup and saucer on the table.

'That's very nice, Sir.'

David thanked her.

'*glebionis segetum*. Corn Marigold.'

Emma smiled shyly.

'It's called Brenanbroi in Gaelic.'

'Is it? Brenanbroi. I will remember that. Thank you.'

'Sir.'

And she left.

~ ~ ~ ~ ~ ~ ~ ~ ~

It was not too long past sunset when they set out for Lochboisdale, but the sky was overcast and the night dark. There was a slight swell which increased as they moved out of the Sound of Barra and to the east of Eriskay. There were six men pulling the oars. Andrew Ferguson and Arthur Morrison were seated together in the stern while David was in the prow, watching the sea as the skiff cut through the waves. Everyone was silent, the mood stern and determined. Dawn was breaking as they cleared the southern tip of South Uist and David could see the cliffs and hear the early morning chorus of the gulls as they swirled and dived overhead. The sun was up when they entered Lochboisdale and David was glad for the heat on his bones after the chill of the night. It was a glorious morning, the light crystal sharp and the air fresh.

They rowed past *The Admiral*, a large transport anchored at the head of the loch. With three masts, a large red funnel and a paddlewheel amidships it was built for transatlantic passage. They rowed close to the ship and David was amazed by its size. It was as if it were alive as it swayed gently in the swell, the boards creaking and straining and the anchor chains singing. He could see sailors quietly about their work high above him, oblivious of the small skiff that made its way towards the jetty. The back of the loch was filled with much smaller vessels, steam ferries like the one that had brought David from Greenock. They stepped ashore and Andrew fell in step with David.

'It's a glorious morning, David, and I believe breakfast has been arranged. We will need it. There's a lot to do.'

At the only inn they were shown to a private room and a table lavishly laid out with chops, bacon, black pudding, eggs and smoked herring. David fell on the food eagerly, the cold night air had made him hungry. As he ate three men arrived and joined the party.

Andrew Ferguson greeted them.

'Gentlemen, I am glad to see that you are all on time. You of course know Reverend Morrison but let me introduce David Wishart. He is here as my assistant representing the interests of Colonel Gordon.'

David was surprised and flattered at such sudden elevation and nodded at the three men with what he felt was a suitable air of gravitas.

'Mr. Wishart, let me introduce Captain Ogilvie of the Argyll militia, Mr. Reynolds who will be in charge of the constables and Captain Arnold of *The Admiral*, the fine vessel that we passed in the mouth of the loch.'

Ferguson pushed his plate to one side.

'Now, gentlemen, we have a lot to organise and time is short. However, it is going to be a long day and you will thankful of this sustenance come the evening.'

He waved his arm over the dishes and the men, accepting his invitation, started filling their plates.

'Captain Ogilvie, we will need the militia in place after the meeting. The meeting will start at midday and I intend that it last no more than an hour. I suggest that you keep the militia below decks until you get word. An hour should be plenty of time for you to surround the building and set up a funnel to direct the tenants to the boats that'll ferry them to *The Admiral*.

Ferguson took a sip from a glass of water. He held it up.

'And this, gentlemen, is all I want your men drinking until after the peasants are safely aboard. The day will provide occasion enough for unpleasantness and conflict and we must remain in control at all times. Donald Nicholson is joining us later. He'll be in the hall and will make a record of those boarding *The Admiral*. No one will leave the hall until Mr. Nicholson has recorded them. Donald, being a local tacksman, knows all the tenants. This will take time and keep the numbers on the harbour at any one time to a minimum. Captain Ogilvie, make certain that you have reliable men on the harbour side as I suspect that there is where trouble may occur. Mr. Reynolds, as they leave the hall the constables will escort the tenants down to the waiting vessels. If any try to break free or refuse to go onto the boats you must use sufficient force to ensure that they comply.'

Reynolds looked up. A slice of bacon speared on his fork was about to enter his mouth.

'Sufficient force?'

'Yes, Mr. Reynolds. Beating, and shackles if necessary. I cannot stress how important it is that these peasants end up on *The Admiral*. And be under no illusions. They'll not want to go. Mr. Wishart will help you supervise the embarkation.'

David had stopped eating. He looked at Reynolds, who returned his gaze with a conspiratorial smile devoid of joy or humour. His face was weather-beaten and the skin stretched taut, his high cheekbones emphasised by his sideburns and his hook nose. The bacon disappeared into his mouth and his fork searched out a mutton chop. Ferguson continued.

'I want you to station constables around Lochboisdale. Reverend Morrison and his men will join you. They have dogs. You will have to chase down any of them foolish enough to flee. And Captain Arnold, I will have clerks on board your ship to take the details of the tenants as they arrive. They will need to sign papers. My men will know what to do. I suggest that this happens on deck before they are taken below. Any questions?'

The meeting continued for an hour with the men fine-tuning the operation. David watched in horror as they discussed the limits to contingency.

'Please, gentlemen, we really do not want any fatalities. It will only make our job all the more difficult.'

He felt overwhelmed, forced to dance to Ferguson's odious tune. Eilidh and her family would be driven and beaten like cattle onto the boats and he would be expected to oversee the brutality. He excused himself and went out for air.

It was still early but the sun heralded a fine day. The streets to the harbour were filling with crofters and cottars. Outside the Town Hall several hundred folk were gathered waiting to be let in. Family met family and children, revelling in the freedom of the unusual, ran around laughing and playing, unaware of their parents' concern. David walked out to the harbour entrance. The hulk of *The Admiral* dominated the skyline and several of the crofters had gone to look, wonder and fear. They watched David with the usual wariness and he couldn't allay their fears with a smile; it was a dishonesty of which he was not capable.

He sat on a rock a little away from the harbour. In the clear air the landscape, harsh, unforgiving and pure, only deepened his sense of despondency. The gulls, carefree, so alive, filled the air with their chatter and cries and in the background the bleating sheep complained of their lot. He looked over to *The Admiral*, its monumental bulk dark and threatening in the morning sun. He thought of Eilidh, her devotion to the landscape she loved, a passion that stilled her poverty and hunger, that signified an ownership more profound than the dry self-interest of the law, his chosen profession.

'Canada is a land of opportunity and limitless possibility. You have a once-in-a-lifetime opportunity to go there and start a new life.'

Ferguson was in full flow, although he had to keep stopping for his words to be translated into Gaelic. David was seated on the stage with Arthur Morrison, Captain Ogilivie in full uniform, Reynolds and Donald Nicholson. From his elevated status on the stage David looked down on the crofters standing quiet but alarmed at what this strange man was suggesting. While the islanders' eyes were riveted on the stage David surveyed the audience looking for Eilidh. The hall was crowded and it was difficult to make out faces that were blocked or staring at the floorboards. Eventually he saw her mother, her face drawn with apprehension and fear, her hand grasping the hand of a child, barely six, who was standing motionless, his sad face focussed on nothing. There was no sign of Eilidh or her sister. Eoin Macdougall was standing next to his daughter-in-law and he caught David's eye with an unforgiving stare. Ashamed, David looked away. He couldn't bear to dwell on the captured audience and his gaze took him through a window to the harbour outside, where he could see the militia taking their places three deep around the Town Hall and down to the jetty. Ferguson was brandishing a piece of paper.

'In my hand I have a letter from Sir John McNeil, the administrator for the poor law in Scotland. He is at present in Canada arranging for the Colonial Authorities to provide transport to your new homes. Each family is guaranteed twenty acres of fine land and generous loans to help you get started. You will be able to banish forever the poverty and famine that has blighted your lives so far. This is an offer you cannot refuse, given you by the generosity of Colonel Gordon, who is paying, out of his own pocket, for your passage.'

The crowd started to grow restless. Some shouted, 'No', 'Never', and 'Barra is our home'.

Andrew Ferguson paused and the crowd quietened. As the door opened and the militia took up places at the back of the hall he took on a sombre tone.

'Barra is no longer your home. South Uist is no longer your home. Colonel Gordon has this day repossessed his lands. You are no longer tenants of the Gordon estates, having forfeited your right by non-payment of rent. Your tenancies have been terminated. When you leave this hall you have only one option; to board *The Admiral* for a new life in Canada. If you do not take this opportunity you will be forced to roam the roads of this land in beggary until you are imprisoned for vagrancy or starvation forces you into the poor house. The constables will escort you to *The Admiral*. I warn you that any disorderliness, lawlessness or attempts at riot will be put down with the full severity of the law.'

The interpreter was looking at Ferguson, finding it hard to comprehend what had been said. Amongst the crowd the few bilingual crofters in quiet tones of shock started explaining what had been said. Ferguson turned to the interpreter.

'For God's sake, man, tell them.'

He turned to his colleagues on the stage.

'Take your stations, gentlemen. Let's get this over with.'

As the interpreter started to explain the situation Ferguson, Morrison, Ogilvie and Reynolds strode purposefully from the stage to a side door. David followed them, aware of the eyes of the crowd upon him.

Once outside Reverend Morrison took his men and their dogs up the only road out of the harbour. The harbour had been built on a peninsular and he stationed himself on its narrowest point. His men had whips and the dogs on leashes were ferocious and excited. Reynolds stopped outside the hall and turned to one of his constables.

'Let them out no more than twenty at time and wait until they are on the boats before the next lot. Any nonsense – ' He brandished his club and the constable smiled.

It seemed like ages before the first group of islanders came out of the hall. They were in family groups, startled and confused; old folk, some walking unsteadily with walking sticks, mothers trying to organise their children, and young men protecting their families, helping dazed, aged mothers along. Many of the old folk and the children were crying while the women tried to calm their fears. As they came down to the jetty David could see the men angry and uncertain, torn between the need to protect their families from violence and the desire to defy the injustice being done to them.

The first group came peacefully enough to the jetty where they were placed in the boats to row them towards *The Admiral.* As the second group made their way to the jetty they could see the boats approaching the hulk of *The Admiral* with their neighbours on board and the full realisation of the betrayal and loss struck home. One old woman threw herself rigid on the ground and screamed in Gaelic, tears streaming down her cheeks. Two of the constables grabbed her and tried to force her up. Her sons ran to her aid and a confrontation was only prevented by the swift intervention of Reynolds who restrained the constables.

'Easy, boys. Easy. Keep your powder dry.'

Two women came and picked the old woman up and led her to the waiting boats. David, stationed near the constables who were directing the families to the boats, could not avoid the distress in the faces of the islanders as they looked out on their ancestral home for the last time. The despair and fear in their eyes shook him to the core. Before this morning David would have considered such savagery by man to fellow man as unimaginable and he watched in disbelief the disinterested efficiency of the constables as they manhandled the strangely quiescent islanders onto the boats. The proceedings took on an unreal air and it may well have remained like that except that, inevitably, three young men with no family or children to restrain them decided to effect an escape. They ran at some of the militia who were caught unawares. The line of militia broke but not before one of the men, barefoot and dressed in a ragged fustian jacket, was beaten to the ground by the butts of the militia rifles. Enraged the militiamen started kicking the fallen man and blood ran from a gash on his face. Some of his relatives ran to his rescue and the militia levelled their rifles. A shot echoed round the hills and all went silent as Ogilvie, his smoking pistol held aloft, strode towards the fallen man who was shaking, his arms covering his face. He placed a foot on the man's shoulder and turned him over.

'Shackle him and get him on the boat.'

His two friends fared no better as they ran into Reverend Morrison and the dogs. They tried to get away over the bare rock that lined the road but were soon brought down by the dogs that drew blood from their legs and tore their trousers to shreds. Morrison had them bound hand and foot and brought down to the harbour on a cart. David watched in horror as, at Morrison's command, his men threw them on the harbour hard and one of his men, with his dog on a leash, stood guard over them.

The forlorn procession of crofters had to make their way to the waiting boats past the two young men trussed and bleeding. David was in turmoil. An old woman blinded by tears was being led by her husband, himself stiff-legged and breathless. She threw herself at a capstan on the harbour wall and, grabbing it, started keening in Gaelic. The old man tried to pick her up but her grief overwhelmed him and he fell in tears by her side. The constables came forward with their clubs and started beating the old couple. David could take it no more and he ran between the constables and the old couple. He ordered the men to go back, and to his surprise they did. Reynolds eyed him dangerously until Ferguson arrived.
'Mr. Reynolds, get your men back in line.'
He turned to David.
'Well done, David. That could have led to a riot. Get the others on the boat. We will deal with these two alone.'
The doors of the hall were locked and the boats rowed out to *The Admiral* as the old woman lay keening, her husband's spare frame trying to protect her.
'All she wants is to be buried with her sons, Wishart. Is that too unchristian for a man of God like yourself? They died in the famine, Mr. Wishart, and she wants to be with them! In God's name, let her be!'

David knew the voice. A small crowd of islanders, exempt from the unforgiving Colonel Gordon in not being his tenants, had gathered to watch the removal of the crofters, some of whom must have been family. They stood a respectful distance behind the militia cordon and in their midst was Dugald. He was pointing a finger at David.

'Are you going to make a painting of this, Mr. Wishart? What will you call it – *The Grieving Mother*?'

The eyes of the crowd settled on David and jeers went up. Ferguson turned to Reynolds.

'Arrest that man.'

'No. Please, no.'

Ferguson ignored David's entreaties and nodded to the eager Reynolds to proceed. He turned to some constables.

'Get them on the boat, and do it quickly.'

In the next group to be released from the hall was Eoin Macdougal's family. He had refused to leave the hall and with his son and Eilidh's mother they were being forcibly marched by the militia to the boats. Behind them a young woman was trying to keep control of several fearful children. Eoin was protesting furiously and his son, refusing to walk, was being dragged along behind him. Eilidh's mother was screaming, trying to break loose from her captors. David went up to Reynolds.

'They cannot go. Their daughters are not with them.'

Reynolds barely registered David's objection.

'That is no concern of mine.'

'But what of their children?'

Reynolds eyed David with scorn and spat on the hard of the jetty. Eilidh's father tried to break free from the militia holding him and in the scuffle Eoin and his son were forced to the ground and handcuffed. Shackles were put round their ankles. They were wrestled into the boats and with a militia guard rowed out to *The Admiral*. Eilidh's mother crumpled weeping on the jetty steps as her men were rowed away. Her despair at the loss of her daughters overwhelmed David and he knew her cries would haunt him. He found himself walking towards Ferguson, who watched David dispassionately as he approached.

'I am sorry, but I cannot be part of this.'

As David turned to walk away Ferguson, smiling kindly, stopped him with a gentle hand on his shoulder.

'That's all right, David. I understand.'

Boats were plentiful in the harbour, drawn by the expectation of a valuable trade, only to be denied the profit of the crofter's return journey, and David had no trouble engaging a fishing smack to sail him back to Barra. It was still light when the vessel cleared the southern tip of Eriskay and turned west to the harbour at Northbay. Barra was shrouded in smoke that hung over the island in layers caught in the still summer air. The evening sun was low in the sky and inflamed the western edges of the hanging smoke a demonic carmine. As the boat neared the shore David could see blackhouses alight the length of the island.

David walked the road to Earsairidh in a daze. The blackhouses were in flames, the reed thatches and timbers having crashed into the body of the dwellings. Cheap crockery and furniture lay scattered around the houses. Rough-hewn tables and chairs lay smashed and burning amongst clothes and wooden buckets, the dignity of a fragile domesticity, painstakingly put together in the face of poverty, summarily destroyed by, David suspected, Balfour and his men. David had wondered why he had not been in Lochboisdale.

As he wandered through the settlements the despoliation of simple honest lives lay all around him. David noticed a crib newly fashioned out of driftwood now halved by the blow from an axe, its cotton hood and a delicately crocheted christening gown lying singed and smoking nearby. And the dogs, loyal to the end to their absent masters, lay slaughtered by their homes.

It was dusk when David reached Earsairidh, the evening made sinister by the silence and the smoke. The blackhouse where he had been offered tea was a shell, the timbers smoking, the frugal comforts of a life of poverty strewn broken around the house. He entered the roofless carcass of the building, the embers of thatch and the timbers glowing in the gloom. On the wall he noticed his picture of Eilidh, pinned proudly by an old nail. Its edges were singed but it had miraculously survived. David took it off the wall and, folding it carefully, placed it in his pocket. He heard crying from the back of the house and coming around the gable end he saw Eilidh. She was standing by her sister who was crouching over the corpse of a collie, stroking its bloodied head, tears streaming down her cheeks. David was about to call her name when Eilidh noticed him. She screamed and grabbed her sister by the arm and together they ran into gathering night, across the heather and into the hills. David called her name but she was gone and he collapsed on the ground, defeated and ashamed at Eilidh's look of terror.

~ ~ ~ ~ ~ ~ ~ ~

'Grandpa, I've found them.'
Lucy was rummaging through an old suitcase that was full of miniature tables, beds and dressers. She handed him a chest of drawers. It had been made with exquisite skill.

The drawers opened with ease, and the top had a walnut veneer.

'Be careful with them, Lucy. They were made by Granny J's father. He was a cabinet maker. He made the table and dresser in our living room. They were a wedding present for me and Grandma when we got married.'

The history excited little interest so David picked up the dolls' house.

'Come on, girls. Let's get this downstairs.'

When he returned for the suitcase of furniture, David carefully placed the pictures back in the portfolio. He paused, holding the portrait of Eilidh, its edges singed and the paper now quite brittle. When he had taken up his living in Govan he had looked for her among the destitute from the highlands and glens who roamed the streets of Glasgow. They had been the lucky ones. The promises of Canadian land had been no more than lies and the papers had reported stories of starvation and death as the Canadian winter took its toll on the penniless emigrants. The Auldearn living went to a local man and Euphemia had broken off the engagement. David had been offered a living in Glasgow, a poor parish, and married Jane, the daughter of an elder. Her generosity of spirit and simple goodness had been his inspiration in a life of service. But the not knowing haunted him and the returning, insistent image of the mother's despair on the jetty at Lochboisdale would allow him no peace.

He placed the picture in the portfolio. A dried and fragile corn marigold, one he must have picked on the machair, had fallen out onto the floor. He picked it up and as he held it in his fingers it crumbled to dust.

The Smile

She heard his boots on the gravel first. It made her look up from her laundry. She hadn't expected him. The old dog growled at him and he struck out at it with his stick. The dog kept its distance, watching the man as he stood in the doorway scowling.

Susan knew no good would come of his visit.

'I told you about that dog.'

Susan dried her hands slowly. She did everything slowly nowadays.

'Good morning, Neil Macleod. What can I do for you?'

It hadn't been the same since David died. Neil Macleod might be the factor but he knew that David was due respect and he had given it him, however reluctantly.

They had had one child, Andrew. He was a good boy but too like his father, proud and principled. When he became a man he had left, like so many of them did. He had made his home in Nova Scotia. He had done well.

He had a wife and three children and it made her sad to think that she would never see them. He wrote once a month but she had to bury David alone. The minister had said kind words and the village had rallied around but she had felt abandoned. It was the first time in her life that she had felt like that, and it was a feeling that had not gone away. The dog was David's dog, a half-breed collie. It was her only companion now.

Neil Macleod was a man of possessions. He was paid well for doing the Campbell's work. He had a big house and his wife wore fine clothes but as the factor he also controlled the possessions of others. In his hands lay the tenants' futures. When contracts were renewed the islanders' livelihood and the very roofs over their heads were in his gift, and contracts were always short on the Isle of Jura.

Neil Macleod sat down at the table, uninvited. He picked up a knife left since breakfast. He inspected it before pushing it to one side.
'Can I make you a cup of tea?'
'It's time for the yearly review.'
Susan sat down at the table.
'I suppose it is. Almost a year since David died.'

They had given up the croft when David took ill. They moved to the cottage; less work, but David had died soon after.

Neil Macleod sat back in the chair and put his thumbs into his waistcoat pockets. He watched her for some moments, making sure she could not avoid his disdain.

'So how are things, Susan?'

'They are fine. The neighbours are very kind.'

He took out a notebook, the one he used to keep a tally of the rents and the estate business. He studied it for some moments before laying the notebook down open on the table. He rubbed his neck as if he had a crick in it.

'You're behind with the rent. And there's the duty work to pay.'

'I'll find it. Don't worry.'

Macleod looked around the cottage, sizing it up.

'It's not the rent I'm worried about.'

Susan looked at the dog. It was lying in the winter sun by the door, eyeing Neil Macleod warily.

'The place is deteriorating. It's too much for a woman alone.'

He raised himself out of his seat and went to the wall and picked at a piece of flaking plaster.

'You know the rules. This isn't your house to let deteriorate. It's owned by Mr. Campbell and you have a duty, Susan, clearly set out.'

From out of his waistcoat pocket he took the blue leaflet.
'In *"The General Conditions and Regulations for the Cottars –"*
'I know the rules, Neil Macleod.'
He continued as if she was a naughty child.
'On the estate of Jura, February 1854.....'

It had started twenty years before – a dispute over duty work. As factor and tacksman Neil Macleod's father, Archibald, collected in the tokens for the *borlanachd*, the duty work each crofter and cottar owed to the Laird. David and Susan were living in a croft at Ardmenish. Their neighbour was Donald Stewart, a blacksmith who chose to pay the fine rather than do the work. It was a large sum – three pounds and eight shillings for the year. David was at the forge when Archibald Macleod came to collect the fine. It was paid in full and he had seen that Archibald Macleod was the worse for the drink, which was not uncommon. Later Archibald claimed that he had never been paid and tried to remove Donald from his forge. David backed Donald's account of the affair. Archibald called them both liars, suggesting that they had split the money between them. The minister intervened by talking to the Campbells and Archibald was made to apologise. David was an elder of the Kirk and Archibald saw conspiracy against him by the sober and God-fearing.

'We need cottars who do the work that is their duty, and not pay the fine. The money is of no use to us at harvest time and when the ditches need dug.'

Susan watched him. There was no point in arguing. The cottage was well kept, better than many.

'I've seen your chickens in the fields and the land in your care is not properly manured.'

'What do you want of me, Neil Macleod?'

'The thatch was due this year and it hasn't been done.'

She wanted to say that she had buried her husband. She wanted to explain that living alone was hard on the spirit as well as the body. She wanted to say that she prayed that he, Neil Macleod, would never have to feel the desolation of bereavement, with your kin far over the sea. But she had her dignity and would not give him the satisfaction of seeing her so lost.

She stood up. She would put an end to it.

'So when do you want me out, Neil Macleod? Tomorrow? Next week?'

'End of the week. You can go to the paupers' cottages at Ardfernal.'

She started to shake. It was a sentence of death. All dignity and independence lost in the company of the simple and the senile. Days spent knitting by the cottage door, of being told what to eat and when to eat it, of being treated like a child.

She felt faint so she grabbed the edge of the table.

In her confusion she thought that he was leaving, but then she noticed he had a rope in his hands.

'For God's sake, not the dog.'

Macleod grabbed the collie by the scruff of the neck and slipped the leash on. At first it struggled, but cowed under a vicious kick.

'Condition six, Susan. "No cottar shall keep a dog". Anyhow, they won't let you keep it in the paupers' cottages.'

'But it's David's dog. I can find it a home.'

'By the weekend.'

He left.

~ ~ ~ ~ ~ ~ ~ ~ ~

She liked to take her chair to the gable end and watch the sun as it set over Beinn an Oir. It was some moment's peace away from the chatter of the other residents.

She took out the photograph. It had come from Canada three days ago. It was heavy, pasted on thick card – the first photograph she had seen of her family. There was Andrew, standing behind his wife who was seated. He looked so much older. He had thickened and his hair was thinning. The woman, Louise, looked severe. She was French. At first that had surprised and worried

Susan; David had feared that she was a Catholic. It turned out that she was not. Her family was from Huguenot stock. The three children were standing in front of their parents. The eldest would be ten now. She searched their sombre faces for a family likeness but she could find none. In a way the photograph made them strangers, unavailable any more to her imaginings. It made her feel more alone.

Maggie came round to sit with her. She liked Maggie over the other residents. She was poor and had remained single, and when her parents died she had been moved to the paupers' cottages. Having had few pleasures in life she was easily content and she enjoyed sitting quietly with Susan.

Susan handed Maggie the photograph.

'My family. In Canada.'

Maggie held it carefully and studied the figures.

'That one's my son, Andrew.'

Susan pointed to him.

'Ay. They're awful bonny. How old's the wee girl?'

Susan had to think.

'Four. Maybe five.'

'Just like the children in the races at the show. Oh, I enjoyed that.'

Maggie chuckled to herself and handed the photograph back.

Holding the photograph, Susan sat quietly looking across Ardfernal towards Beinn an Oir. She thought of the annual Jura Show.

She had always gone with David but this year she and Maggie had walked to the show, past the old cottage. The roof had been burnt. Susan noticed some of the adjacent crofts had been abandoned and were derelict as well.

'Isn't that a shame, Susan? They do it for the deer.'

She hadn't told Maggie it was her cottage.

She had sat with Maggie on a gentle rise above the show pens and the field laid out for the children's sports. They sat on a tartan rug they had brought with them and drank the water they had carried in an old milk bottle. A marquee had been erected and the space around it roped off. Inside were all the cups and plaques to be presented by Mrs. Campbell to the winners. Susan noticed the Minister and the local doctor mixing with the Campbells' friends. They always seemed to have visitors during the week of the show. It was all very grand, with the maids walking round with plates of food and drink.

They watched the judging of the livestock and the children's races. Susan had wondered if Andrew's children, she didn't feel that they were her grandchildren, she wondered if they ran races at school, if they were clever and brave. Andrew mentioned their health and how tall they were in his letters, but little else.

During the show a few old neighbours had come to say hello. Only Sally, David's cousin, had stayed for a natter. Their anger at Susan's eviction had soon dissipated and the neighbours' visits to the paupers' cottages had ceased once the spring planting started.

She saw Neil Macleod standing outside the marquee. He was talking and laughing with the other factors and the ghillies. He was smartly dressed in his tweeds.

She was watching the children's sack race down below when she noticed the dog. It was a young spaniel looking at her with its tail wagging. Susan offered her hand and the wee dog scampered up to get its ears tickled. He jumped up on his hind legs and started licking Susan's hand

'Walter, stop that and come here.'

Susan looked up. It was Mrs. Campbell. She was accompanying the livestock judge back to the marquee. She was elegant and beautiful, dressed in a dark blue suit with a silk blouse.

'I'm terribly sorry. You must not mind him. He's a little devil.'

And she smiled at Susan, a smile of genuine warmth.

The dog had gambolled to the new distraction of his mistress and with the slightest nod of the head to Susan and Maggie, Mrs. Campbell was gone.

Maggie had nudged Susan.

'Well.'

It had been a nice smile. A genuine smile. Not one of those forced grimaces of her husband trying to contain his disregard.

The evening was still and the sun had gone.

'Mrs. Campbell looked lovely today.'

Maggie nodded.

'She's always so elegant. Such a lovely smile. You know she sends us a cake every Christmas. Baked in the big house.'

The friends sat silently in the peace of the evening as the sky darkened and the clouds turned orange and grey.

The Locket

Chrissie MacLean had heard that he had returned and that he was safe and in one piece, and she was glad. She had heard it first from Mary. She had met her on the road.

'He was with the other lads, talking by the harbour wall. I swear he's taller and bigger than when he went.'

That was a week ago. It hurt her that he hadn't come to see her. She had written to him regularly and had sent socks and gloves that she had knitted. At first there were postcards in his tentative hand, brief and embarrassed and then no more. This didn't worry her.

'I'm no good at writing, and there's not the time.'

That was on his first leave. He had seemed withdrawn and unsure. His bright smile had deserted him and even his brown curls had been sacrificed to the regimental barber. He hadn't come back after that He spent his leaves in Glasgow with an uncle and eventually in France, choosing not to come home. She had continued to write with news from the island. His mother got the odd short letter, full of bland reassurances, saying nothing. Chrissie hadn't seen him for three years.

She had thought of visiting his family's croft but things were busy on the farm and, anyway it seemed too forward.

On the Saturday, she went to Castlebay with her mother. They met Morag MacNeil and Caroline MacKinnon and were talking outside 'The Island Store' when they saw him. Morag noticed him first. He was at the pier, smoking a cigarette, watching the men on the ferry unload boxes of groceries and barrels of beer.

'Why, isn't that John Buchanan? I heard he was back.'

They all turned to look in the direction of her gaze, just as he flicked the butt end of his cigarette into the sea and Chrissie recognized his profile. He hadn't smoked before.

'It must be good to have him back, Chrissie.'

Kate MacLean saw her daughter's confusion.

'Oh, he's been too busy to bother with us out at Tangasdal.'

'Well, his mother must be thanking God he's back and safe.'

It was Caroline. There was an awkward pause. Kate broke the tension.

'Well, we must be getting on. Are you going to the dance?'

Mother and daughter walked back in silence to avoid the obvious topic. At the croft the routine of the day's chores and her father's concern for a calf pushed Chrissie's disappointment into the background. It was later that night, as she was sitting by the fire darning Calumn's sweater, her brother was a lad of careless energy, that she thought of John and seeing him standing on the pier. It startled her to think that if Morag hadn't recognised him Caroline would probably not have noticed him there. She had followed Morag's gaze and briefly, for less than a second, had been looking for someone else. He had changed. She had watched him while the other women talked. There was something unfamiliar in his manner, the way he stood, the way he moved, something distant, almost supercilious. There was no question of Chrissie going down to greet him. There had been a time when she would have known he was there before seeing him, when she would have run up to him knowing she would be greeted by a laugh and smile.

She gazed at the peat smouldering in the hearth and a sadness filled her. Somehow she had feared something would be lost when they said farewell on the pier. He was excited, joking and joshing with the three pals, Donald

McNeil, Roderick Fraser and Christopher MacPherson. It was the great adventure, the unknown that held him that day. The farewell and the kiss had been awkward, getting in the way of the onward journey. She had said that she would wait for him, that he was the only one for her. She gave him a locket with a curl of her hair. He had smiled and told her not to be silly. The four of them had clambered on the ferry with an excitement that excluded her. She cried as the ferry left the bay and with Janet Gilles ran around the headland to Rubha Charnain and stood watching the ferry till the mist took it.

Her father came in from the byre and sat heavily in his chair by the fire. Chrissie put her knitting down and, taking the kettle from the hob, poured the boiling water into the waiting teapot. She looked out of the window, across the dunes and to the sea. Its immensity always scared her and made her glad of the fields and hills, this little piece of the stable and familiar the Lord had given her. The horizon glowed with the orange and greys of dusk. The nights were drawing out.

She was moving sheep from the hillside of Beine na Moine down to the dry stone field near the croft as they would be lambing soon. The sheep, scenting the fresh grass, were noisily drifting along the gravel road when she saw him. He was strolling down the road towards her; she guessed he had been visiting the burial ground. She stopped and the sheep fell to grazing. He looked uncertain as he approached; the old familiarity had gone. He stopped several paces from her and nodded.

'I've been visiting the grave.'

'Aye. I'm sorry. You were close.'

John blinked as if trying to wipe away an irritating emotion.

'He was old.'

It was the voice of a stranger, cold and remote.

'He was a good man. Kind.'

John watched her as if she were a simpleton, an object of pity.

'Remember when he took us fishing?'

He looked away. Chrissie had crossed a line, into a familiarity he didn't want to share. They were silent for a while. Chrissie looked down to evade his enquiring stare. The sheep were getting restless. She smiled at him.

'I need to get on.'

He nodded.

'Will I see you at the dance?'

'Aye.'

She stood to one side as he passed on his way to Castlebay.

Mary had been right. He had filled out, his features had coarsened, his jowls were heavy and his mouth turned down. But it was his eyes that saddened her. They were guarded and calculating, and she shivered at the thought of what they had seen.

Her mother was making bannocks when Chrissie entered the croft carrying a creel of peat for the fire.
'I saw you speaking to John Buchanan.'
Chrissie nodded.
'What did he have to say for himself?'
'He had been to the grave.'
'Is that all?'
Chrissie put the creel by the fire.
'He hasn't the courtesy to visit. You were betrothed.'
'We weren't.'
'It was understood.'
Chrissie brushed her hands on her skirt.
'Things change, mother.'
Katie looked at her daughter, wanting the anger and the pride, but Chrissie picked up a pail.
'I must see to the chickens.'

She had danced with Sheila McNeil twice and with Calumn and with her father. The few young men were gathered at the back chatting. John was there; he hadn't danced all evening. The young men were talking to him – the hero returned from the war. She noticed that he was listening, saying little as those too young to have joined the fight tried to impress. Roderick Fraser asked for a dance. He had been dancing with Janet all evening. He was the one who had returned, glad to be home. He had bought the ring in Glasgow and on his return, leaving the ferry, had gone to see Janet first. He and Chrissie danced the *Gay Gordons;* his steps were nimble and there was happiness in his eyes. He had been the frail, quiet one of the quartet that set out four years before, but as they danced Chrissie realised that he was the one with the strength to return undefeated by the horrors that she could barely imagine. Donald McNeil was dead and Christopher McPherson, in a hospital in Glasgow, was contemplating life from a wheelchair. They turned neatly and Roderick swept Chrissie round as the music stopped. He bowed in thanks and caught Chrissie looking over at John.

'It's not easy for him, Chrissie.'

'Why? I want to know.'

Roderick paused, considering his answer.

'He and Donald were very close.'

The music started up and the dancers began to line up for *Strip the Willow.* Chrissie found a chair on the edge of the dance floor and through the frantic and laughing lines of dancers watched John. The young men talked to him but he was apart, listening and nodding but, hands in pockets, his eyes swept the room as if watching a scene that was strange and incomprehensible to him. The chaotic energy of *Strip the Willow* gave way to a slow waltz and as the younger dancers caught their breath the dance floor entertained sedate elderly couples. Chrissie got up and walked across the hall towards John. She knew that eyes were on her, that she was the centre of attention. John watched her approach. Chrissie smiled and as she took his arm said quietly.

'Dance with me, John Buchanan. You owe me that.'

As they danced his step was firm and sure and as the walls of the hall swirled round Chrissie's spirits rose; it was as it was before. When the music stopped she kept hold of his hand.

'Come with me, John.'

To her surprise he followed out of the hall, meek as a lamb. They walked for a while hand in hand and then Chrissie turned to face him.

'I love you, John Buchanan. I always have, and I always will. I want to be your wife.'

His grip relaxed and she let go of his hand. He was silent as if trying to find an impossible form of words that could say, kindly, what he didn't want to say.

'It cannot be, Chrissie. I'm sorry, and it's not your fault, but it is not possible.'

She looked at him. There were tears in his eyes.

'Why? Is there someone else?'

John was silent.

'Why, John? What have I done wrong?'

He looked out across the bay and then back at Chrissie.

'There is no-one else and you've done nothing wrong.'

He paused as if summoning up his strength.

'I'm leaving tomorrow. I won't be back. It's best this way, believe me.'

'But why? Why?'

But he had turned and walked away into the Hebridean night.

And so it was. John Buchanan left the next day and Chrissie never saw him again. Janet and Roderick were married and Chrissie was godmother to their firstborn son, David. But men were scarce on the island after the war and it was left to the small boy to satisfy her maternal instincts. Three years went by with no news and then the letter came to the Buchanan household. It was from a coroner. John had died, an accident at work, and was buried in Glasgow.

~ ~ ~ ~ ~ ~ ~ ~

Chrissie walked up the path of the hospital. On the lawns on either side young men were sitting quietly in wheelchairs enjoying the sun. A handsome young man gave her a cheery 'Hello' as she passed him making his awkward way on a prosthetic leg. Christopher was seated in a wheelchair in the day room. His grey trousers were wrapped around what was left of his legs, amputated several inches above the knee. He smiled when he saw Chrissie and waved although he was the only one in the room.

'Hello, Chrissie. It's good to see you.'

'Hello, Christopher.'

His face was gaunt and there was a livid scar down the side of his cheek. She had thought through this meeting to prepare herself at seeing him so broken. She hoped that the horror she felt was not as obvious as she feared it must be.

'Don't worry, Chrissie. It's OK. I never was a ladies' man.'

An involuntary laugh broke the tension and for a moment he was the young lad who had gone to war, the joker, shy and sensitive, who sent himself up to hide his awkwardness.

'These are from your mother.'

She handed him a parcel – some woollens and a cake.

'She told me to tell you she wants you to come home.'

'I know. I know. I'm best off here at present. They take good care of me. At least as long as the guilt lasts.'

His laugh was dry and bitter.

'How are you, Chrissie? You look well.'

'Things are good at the croft. Calumn is quite the big lad now. He helps father. He's clever, too. Mother says, too clever.'

'That's good.'

He asked after mutual friends and news from Northbay. Chrissie showed him a photo of Roderick and Janet, Roderick holding a newly-born David. Christopher looked at it for a long time, his eyes seemed to explore every moment of the photograph, and his face softened. He handed it back.

'No, keep it. It's for you.'

He smiled and kept it in his hand like a precious relic.

'David's much bigger now, walking and gabbling away.'

They fell silent. Christopher stared at the photograph. The silence became awkward and Christopher looked out of the window and then at Chrissie.

'You want to know about John. That's why you're here.'

Chrissie nodded.

'It's maybe best left ,Chrissie. You don't need to know.'

'I do, Christopher, or I'll not be able to rest.'

He returned his gaze to the photograph which he held in both hands.

'He never stopped loving you, Chrissie. It was always you.'

'I don't believe you. I told him I wanted to be his wife. I would have gone anywhere for him. He knew that.'

'I know.'

'Then why did he abandon me?'

Christopher gazed out of the window and then down at the photograph. He placed the photograph on the table by his chair. His face was troubled and as Chrissie watched him she became afraid.

'He killed himself.'

'What.'

'He shot himself.'

'Oh, my God. My God.'

Chrissie could feel herself trembling

'The accident, it wouldn't have been fair on his parents, and the authorities don't like their heroes committing suicide. You know they gave him a medal, the MC, for bravery. He threw it in the Clyde.'

Christopher paused. Chrissie was numb with shock. He stretched out a hand to hers and she seemed to come to.

'Why? Why did he kill himself?'

'He couldn't live with what he had become.'

'I don't understand.'

Christopher closed his eyes and his hands clasped round each other. Chrissie noticed that he had started to shake as if he was cold.

'The trenches do things to you. We all changed more than we understood. We didn't notice it while we there.'

His eyes grew troubled.

'The three of us were together. Donald, John and me. We had been over the top before. We reckoned we were lucky. We were running across no-man's land when a mortar exploded near us. We were blown into a shell hole. John was OK but my legs had gone. Donald was in a bad way.'

Christopher stopped and seemed to stare into the past.

Chrissie wanted to tell him to stop but knew it was too late; the story had to be finished.

'I don't remember much. We were there for quite a while. John told me later that he knew Donald was dying. I was bleeding badly. We were under fire but John knew he had to do something so he put me across his shoulders and ran back to our trench. I would have died if he hadn't done that. The attack had been a disaster and they had sounded the retreat. They wouldn't let him go back for Donald. He said...'

Christopher stopped and looked at Chrissie.

'I need to know it all.'

'He said he heard his screams all night.'

Chrissie's eyes closed and her hands tore at her handkerchief. She nodded.

'Go on.'

'I heard from the other lads that John had gone wild. It happened sometimes, the death wish, trench fever, guilt, despair any number of horrors. He would throw himself into battle just hoping to die. In the heat of the battle you do terrible things, Chrissie.'

Christopher paused looking at his hands. He continued quietly

'Terrible things. It's then the trenches take you. They make you their own. Nowhere else is real. Nowhere else makes sense and it's only your pals who understand. They are the only people you can stand to be around. Going home becomes the nightmare.'

He lent back in his chair.

'People think that because the fighting has stopped and the war is over that the lads can return back to their old lives. It's not like that. As you can see.'

Christopher nodded towards the scene outside and the wheelchairs on the grass.

'But for some, the wounds you can't see.'

He stopped. And for a while they sat in silence. Chrissie wanted it to end but knew that she could not hide from the awful truth, not now.

'He used to come and see me. We were old pals, you didn't have to explain. He told me that he was no longer any good for you. He wanted to spare you what he had become.'

Chrissie started to weep quietly. Christopher took the locket out of his pocket and handed it to her.

'He always loved you, Chrissie. He was wearing this when he died.'

Chrissie shook her head.

'Why? Why?'

'He wasn't well, Chrissie. He had rages, there was a terrible anger in him and he took to the drink. The night he killed himself he had been drinking and he got into a fight. He often did. This time he almost killed a lad; it took several men to pull him off. The trenches had claimed him. He knew he couldn't live a normal life anymore. Normality mocked him and what he had become. He hated himself and he hated the world he couldn't be part of.'

Chrissie stood by the grave. It was a simple granite cross engraved *Cpl. John Buchanan MC 1898 – 1923.* The graveyard was surrounded by mean and cramped houses and in the distance she could see an iron foundry. The noise of industry filled the still spring air made yellow by a pall of smoke that gave off an acrid smell. This was nowhere for him to rest. On his grave she put a small bouquet of yellow irises and montbretia, island colours, and prayed for his soul to be at peace.

Tha 'n t-anam truagh a nis fo sgaoil
An taobh a muigh dh' an chaim;

A Chrisosd chaoimh nam beannachd soar
Cuartaich mo ghaol 'na aim.*

The Gaelic caused a passing couple to look over. They smiled sadly and hurried on their way.

~ ~ ~ ~ ~ ~ ~ ~

The grass on the machair had started to grow in the gentle spring warmth and in the bright sunlight the harebells, trefoil and thrift painted the machair with colour. It was a breezy cloudless day and the sea in the shallows was an inviting sapphire blue which seemed to shine with the white of the surf as the waves busily lapped the shore. The kelp thrown up by last night's storm lay in vast brown mounds and Chrissie was cutting it and forking it into the cart. David, his arms full of the slippery brown seaweed, was helping out with the brief enthusiasm of an eight-year-old.

She toiled for several hours and then, with the cart full, Chrissie rested. David by now was running in and out of the surf with the young half-breed collie, his constant companion. She watched him as he stopped and, shielding his eyes from the late afternoon sun, gazed out across the limitless ocean. Chrissie called him over and they shared some oatcakes and cold tea while David talked about the croft, school and aeroplanes, explaining that a woman had flown from London to Australia all on her own. Chrissie half listened, enjoying his youthful curiosity as it rushed from one urgent topic to another.

Chrissie collected the pony that was grazing on the machair and hitched her back on the cart. David, talking all the while, held the reins as they walked back up the path towards the small township. At the crossroads he met his two sisters and with a confident informality that had no need of goodbyes ran off with them to his croft, chased all the while by the barking of his collie.

Taking the reins Chrissie guided the pony in the opposite direction to where her father and Callumn were digging the lazybeds.

The poor soul is now set free
Outside the soul-shrine;
O kindly Christ of the free blessings
Encompass Thou my love in time.

The prayer *Tha 'n t-anam truagh a nis fo sgaoil* is from the *Carmina Gadelica* by Alexander Carmichael (1900)

The Gift

He had always thought of himself as a modern man. He understood the newfangled things. He had spent hours under the bonnet of Robert Shaw's car until he knew how it worked. The old folk had looked askance when the crane on the Clyde steamer had lowered the car gently onto the pier at Craighouses.

'What's wrong with the feet God gave us?'

'The road will shake it to bits, you see.'

And when Robert had started it up the noise had alarmed the adults and frightened the children.

'It'll scare the sheep and cattle. Put the chickens off their lay.'

But Duncan had been fascinated. One day he would have a motor car.

He picked up his cas-chrom. The six-foot oak haft was worn smooth with use. To be able to dig its large metal blade into the soil and turn a clod of earth was a skill all islanders had to learn. At the age of eight he would take an old broken cas-chrom and follow his father, imitating his digging action. He would put his bare foot on the peg at the end of the haft, dig the right-angled blade into the earth and then heave with all his juvenile might, the haft swinging wildly above his head like a tree in a gale. With his father's help he soon mastered the technique and by the age of twelve could turn a line of heavy ground in good time.

Duncan drove the blade into last year's hard earth and with a quick sideways jerk turned the sod over. It was hard work and the soil offered little reward; not enough to buy a car. The day was beautiful, though, and the spring colours of the celandine and primroses on the edge of the Long Rigs shone in the April sunlight. There was not a cloud on the majestic peak of Beinn An Oir and the skylarks were singing in the heavens. On days like this there was nowhere in God's creation more beautiful. But as Duncan worked, his wrists turning the cas-chrom, tossing the sods of earth over to his left, he felt a great discontent. This pauper's work was all he had to look forward to until he became old and his hopes and dreams became buried in this landscape. He rested on the haft and looked across the Sound of Jura to the gentle hills of Knapdale on the mainland. In the clear spring air they appeared unusually close. Duncan's eye followed the Clyde steamer from Glasgow as it made its way up the Sound of Jura. It would call in at Craighouses bringing the mourners to the funeral of Alastair Buie the day after tomorrow.

Alastair's death had only intensified Duncan's restlessness. The old man had taught Duncan the fiddle. His playing was known throughout the islands; his style had set him apart. Many fiddlers tried to outplay each other with speed and virtuosity. At the dances in Bowmore they would set the hall alight with their wizardry, but that was not Alastair's way.
'Play to the tune, lad, play to the tune. You are telling a story, not running a race.'
Alastair had a tone that no fiddler could match. Airs would become pure poetry when he played them and jigs and reels were fluid and seamless; the old tunes born anew under his delicate hands, and what hands. Sitting in the old man's croft of an early evening Duncan would watch Alastair play. His large hands, fresh from an afternoon's cutting peat or fighting the plough, caressed the strings of the old fiddle, coaxing out tunes that would make you cry or dance.

Duncan's mother had been left her father's fiddle. She had played as a young woman but five children and a crofting life had left it to gather dust. He didn't know why, but Duncan was always drawn to the instrument. He had badgered his mother until she taught him the rudiments. Being young he had no thought of failure, only enthusiasm, and by the age of eight he could hold a tune learnt by ear.

As they were friends, Alastair would call by to talk to Duncan's father, John, and the small boy would show off. Alastair would tousle Duncan's curly hair, saying he had a fine arm on him. Duncan was persistent and by the age of ten he would go in the evening to Alastair's croft and they would play together, he on his mother's fiddle and Alastair on 'the sweet one' handed down through so many generations, no one knew how old it was.

The steamer pulled in at the pier. It would be bringing Neil, Alastair's grandson. Five years ago Neil had escaped. He made good money working in the shipyards on the Clyde. He would be dressed in fine clothes and with money to impress the girls. Neil would have a car.

The sun was getting low on the horizon and Duncan still had several rows to finish.

That evening Duncan went to the Hotel in Craighouses. He could tell the difference before he entered. The usual hum of conversation and laughter had been replaced by a single harsh voice. Neil was at the bar. He had filled out, his hair was neatly cut and slicked back and he had grown a moustache just like the film stars sported. The men in the bar were listening to him as they would to a stern preacher or the baillie at rent time. It was almost as if they were intimidated, in awe of this strange man returned to their midst. Neil seemed unaware of this distance or, if he was aware, he was enjoying it, taking it as a sign of adulation and respect.

'Ah, a Saturday night. You've seen nothing like it. The dance halls filled with beautiful women. And the drinking. You wouldn't believe it.'

His voice had changed; the mocking harsh tones of the city had coarsened his island lilt. He was louder, more confident, aggressive like the men from the city, the ones who worked the boats and occasionally came to the dances at Bowmore.

The following morning was overcast. Duncan was working the Long Rigs, digging the potato rows. He had been working for four hours when he saw Neil make his way along the road from Keils. He was wearing a smart tweed jacket and Oxford bags with a knife-sharp crease. His smart shoes were shiny. Duncan looked down at his working boots with their improvised laces and his patched working trousers. He felt ashamed.

Neil leant with his back to the stone wall. He took out a cigarette and lit it while watching Duncan work. When he had finished the row Duncan joined Neil, cleaning the metal blade with a trowel as he walked over. Neil took the cas-chrom from Duncan and inspected it, making sure not to dirty his clothes.

'You're awful skilful turning the sod. As good as my father.'

He looked at the cas-chrom as if it was a loaded gun.

'You'd better look out or you will end your days with one of these in your hands.'

Duncan took the tool back and rested the long haft against the wall. Neil gave him a cigarette.

'How's Glasgow?'

'Great. Really great.'

'No, what's it really like?'

'Not like here.'

Duncan turned away, offended by the evasion. He looked across to the Paps, covered in cloud.

'You can be your own man in the city. Here if you go with a girl they will have you down the aisle in a week and the minister will never let you forget.'

'Have you been with a girl?'

Neil's laugh annoyed Duncan; it made him feel childish and naïve.

'I've had lots of women. It's different over there.'

They smoked in silence. Duncan tried to imagine the city that the minister called Gomorrah and he felt unsettled.

'Why do you think people leave this island? They've been doing it for centuries. How many relatives do you have in America? Or Canada?

Duncan shrugged. More than he could recollect.

'Why do you think they left?'

The question was an accusation to all who remained, those who doffed their caps, paid unfair rents and were reliant on the good will and whim of the landlords.

'I've got cousins in America. They farm six hundred acres. They own the land, Duncan. They don't answer to anyone.'

Neil dropped his cigarette and ground it with the sole of his brown and cream correspondent shoe.

'I'll be going.'

'To America?'

Neil laughed again.

'Of course.'

'When?'

'Soon. When I've got the passage.'

Duncan considered this prospect. America. That would be fine, the land of sunshine and opportunity. But then he thought of his mother's tears. And then there was Alice.

Duncan turned the cas-chrom around in his hands.

The silence returned and Neil lit another cigarette.

'Do you have a car?'

Neil laughed. 'What would I want a car for? In Glasgow? No, I'm saving for the passage.'

Neil patted Duncan on the shoulder.

'I'd better leave you to it. Will I see you tonight?'

'Maybe.'

Duncan watched Neil as he strolled down the track towards the Corran River. As his friend disappeared behind the crofts that lined the road, Duncan returned to the field. The visit had unsettled him. Neil had made him feel unsophisticated, a simpleton. There was something about him that made Duncan uneasy. He was not the friend of old; the intimacy had been lost somewhere in the bustle and noise of the city. To his alarm Duncan realised that he watched his old friend from the same fearful distance as did the old men in the bar last night.

Duncan didn't go to the Hotel that night. There were things to do on the croft. His mother Catherine was busy baking for the funeral so Duncan and his father had the milking to do and the chickens to coop for the night.

They were taking the cows back to the pasture.

'That Neil is quite a man now, isn't he?'

'I suppose he is.'

'Dressed like one of those American film stars, and with money to burn.'

Duncan let the comment pass as he took the chain off the gate. As he chivvied the cows through he was aware of his father watching him like a hawk.

After supper Duncan took his mother's fiddle down and practiced a few sets for the funeral. Archie Lindsay would play the pipes over the grave and lead the mourners back to the village hall, but Duncan would be expected to play at the wake.

Sandy MacDonald had arrived from Skye. He was staying with Mary, Alastair's widow, at the croft at Keils. He was a great fiddler and had made records. He would be playing at the wake and the thought of it made Duncan nervous.

'So, you will be playing with the great Sandy MacDonald tomorrow night.'

Catherine smiled at her son.

'Maybe. He will probably play on his own.'

'Of course you will. Your grandfather would be proud.'

Duncan looked at the fiddle. It was fair, with a nice tone, but secretly Duncan hankered after a better instrument, one that would be his own. But he kept these thoughts to himself for fear of offending his mother.

The men were bareheaded, dressed in grey and black. The women wore shawls over their heads. The day was overcast with the threat of rain. A chair had been brought for Mary and she sat surrounded by her children and grandchildren at the graveside.

It had happened quickly; a chill caught during the spring planting had turned into pneumonia. The pipes of Archie Lindsay filled the glen and rolled up the heather to the Paps. As Duncan watched the coffin being lowered he realised for the first time that he would not play with the old man again. He looked across at Mary. Her face was set stern, her hand grasping the hand of her eldest son Callum who was standing behind her. Duncan noticed that her knuckles had turned white with the holding and Callum's other hand gently came to rest on his mother's shoulder.

As was the way there were no prayers for the deceased; the minister read from the Bible for the instruction of the living. The men drank a round of whisky and then oatcakes and cheese were eaten. The cemetery was to the north of the township of Keils. The crofting families of the Buies, Darrochs and Keiths had laid their folk to rest here for generations, next to the high and mighty Campbells. As the mourners made their way down to the township the mood lightened as folk started talking. Hushed, of course, and respectful, the laughter and gossip would come later. Duncan walked down with Alice. She was quiet. Alastair had been her neighbour, as much a father as the one that she had lost at the age of four.

Neil caught up with them, hands in his pockets. He turned and smiled.

'I can't wait for the music. Will you give me a dance tonight, Alice?'

She smiled shyly.

'I'll hold you to that.'

He laughed and sauntered off.

Duncan looked at Alice as her gaze followed Neil.

'He's quite the man now, isn't he?'

She smiled, still watching Neil as he disappeared into Mary's croft.

'Isn't he just.'

It was only family that paid their last respects at the croft. The rest of the community made their way along the shore to the village hall at Craighouses. They walked slowly as if reluctant to let the old fiddler go. The talk was subdued. Alice was silent, tied up in her own thoughts and memories and Duncan, walking by her side, knew not to intrude. He wondered if he knew her too well, yet not well enough. Somehow they had grown up with the assumption that they would marry. They had always been friends; he knew what she thought of things, what made her angry and made her laugh. She knew how not to annoy him and what made him happy. It had all seemed so simple. But with the death of Alastair and the return of Neil things had changed. Walking by Alice's side it was like they were a married couple, but they had never had the mystery, or the romance. He thought of Neil's easy way and his experience with women and the fact that he, Duncan, had never kissed Alice, never really kissed her like they did in the films. The knowledge that he could never admit this to Neil made Duncan feel awkward, almost ashamed.   Each wrapped up in their own thoughts they entered the village hall. Alice joined Catherine in the kitchen, helping to put out the plates and making tea.

Sandy MacDonald was seated on the stage talking to Tam, the accordion player from Ardlussa in the north of the island. Tam and Alastair had played at the local dances for as long as most folk could remember. Sandy was tall and grey-haired and Duncan, who had only heard him on the radio, realised that he was the same age as Alastair. Tam called Duncan over.
'This is Duncan McLean. He plays the fiddle.'
Duncan shook hands with Sandy. He was smartly dressed, with neatly-cut hair and a crisp white shirt set off with gold cuff-links and a tartan tie. The effortless elegance and grace that hung round him like an expensive cologne made Duncan so nervous that he fumbled opening the old violin case .

'I thought we'd start with *Captain Campbell's Strathspey* and follow it with the *The Waverley Ball*. They're fine tunes. Alastair loved playing them.'

Duncan nodded. Sandy's confidence in Duncan's ability made him all the more nervous.

Tam agreed.

'Ay. We'll keep it jolly at first. Alastair was a man for a dance.'

Sandy wrote out a running order of agreed sets and some solo pieces for himself. Duncan was glad that he wasn't asked to do a solo. They tuned up and, seated on the stage, the trio watched the hall fill up.

Reverend Robertson joined them on the stage and honoured the memory of Alastair with fond anecdotes, grateful for the memories of a generous man. Shrouded by her black shawl, Mary listened with a smile verging on tears, the warmth of the community keeping the chill of loss at bay. Duncan noticed Neil and Alice together. He was whispering in her ear during the Minister's speech, making her giggle guiltily. His arm had snaked around her waist.

Duncan played at Sandy's bidding. The older man had an elegance and sure touch to his playing, the product of a lifetime performing. It was easy for Duncan to follow him so while he played he watched the dance floor. Neil and Alice always started the sets together and he held her close during the polkas and waltzes. Distracted, Duncan's attention wandered and twice he almost missed a change.

There was a pause and Tam called Duncan over.

'Concentrate. This is no way to see Alastair off.'

Sandy came over.

'Give us one of your best strathspeys, my lad.'

He patted Duncan on the back and left the stage.

Duncan was at a loss. Tam played the opening bars of *The Miller o' Drone* and Duncan took up the melody. He played well, for the memory of Alastair. Sandy joined him on the stage for the last few bars and without a pause went at a furious pace straight in to a set of jigs. Duncan became aware of a commotion at the back of the hall, of dancers slowing up and heads turning. Sandy nodded at Tam and they switched to *Maggie Brown*, the tune that Sandy had made his own on radio and record. The audience started clapping in time and the disturbance was forgotten. As the last notes echoed into the night they broke for an interval. Sandy put his arm round Duncan.

'Well played, lad.'

He nodded to the back of the hall.

'Don't worry about that. Young men and drink. You have to play through it.'

During the interval the warm babble of conversation and laughter filled the hall, life after death. Duncan was worried about Alice. There was no sign of her or Neil. His conversation with Neil the previous day came back. Duncan's eyes roamed around the hall trying to find Alice. Neil was a charmer. *I've had lots of women.* His words and their heartlessness panicked Duncan. He felt a hand on his shoulder. It was Sandy.

'Duncan, Mary wants a word with you.'

Duncan came to. Mary, frail and small, was standing between Sandy and Callum. Her hand gently touched Duncan's face.

'Alastair said you were to have this. He said only you could play it.'

Callum had Alastair's fiddle, 'the sweet one', in his hand. He offered it to Duncan. The room was silent. Mary smiled.

'It's yours now.'

At first Duncan didn't understand. His mind was still on Alice, but as Callum placed the fiddle in Duncan's hands the enormity of the gift struck him like a blow. He looked at Mary. Behind her smile was a desolation and loss near to breaking her, and Duncan understood that he had to take the burden and privilege of the fiddle to ease Mary's pain. The sorrow at Alastair's death, at the end of the music, the sorrow that he had put to one side in the newness of death and the flurry of the funeral, all threatened to overwhelm him, and his eyes filled with tears. He took the fiddle. It was worn and scratched in places but it felt warm in his hands.

As Duncan always told it, and there was no reason to doubt him, the rest was a blur. The fiddle was tuned, Sandy had seen to that. Duncan walked to the stage alone, aware only of the fiddle in his hands. He didn't think of what to play. He didn't decide what to play. He just played. It was as if the spirit of the fiddle, of the hundreds of years and thousands of tunes it had played, had taken him over.

Those in the audience that night said that they had never heard anything like it. He started with the slow air, *McCrimmon's Lament*. It was more than music. It was the spring air on the Paps, and the clear light across the water to the mainland. It was the steps of the dance through the ages and the lonely call of the sheep on a spring evening. Time stood still, and the shy young man was transformed, some said, possessed. For two hours he played without stopping, airs, jigs and reels, the intensity of his playing building with each tune. He ended with *Aldavalloch*, played with a passion that left Duncan drained. Catherine said it was a relief when he stopped; she was afraid for her son. He lowered the fiddle and looked at the audience as if for the first time.

The evening was over and the hall reluctantly cleared. Alice was at the back of the hall with Morag, her mother. Duncan went to her.

Morag took the fiddle from Duncan and looked at it as if it held a secret.

'You played well, Duncan.'

She returned the fiddle.

'Take my daughter home. I have to clear up.'

They walked in silence along the shore to Keils. Alice took Duncan's hand.

'Why so quiet? You were marvellous tonight.'

'Was I?'

'Of course you were. I was so proud of you.'

'What about Neil?'

Alice stopped. She looked at Duncan the way the schoolmistress had when he had got his sums wrong.

'Neil.'

She laughed gently.

'He's hopeless. He got drunk and started a fight with the Shaw boys. His father had to take him outside. His father was fit to kill him.'

'But you were dancing with him.'

'He's not the man he says he is, Duncan. He lives in a hostel and works on the docks when he's lucky.'

She laughed.

'God, do you think I would prefer him over you?'

The accusation left Duncan speechless.

'I love you, Duncan McLean. I always have.'

And she kissed him. She kissed him the way they did in the films.

As he dug the rows on the Long Rigs Duncan watched the progress of the Clyde steamer up the Sound of Jura and into Craighouses. Families would be on the pier seeing off their loved ones, waving their reluctant goodbyes. And then there would be Neil, cowering from his father's silent fury until he could escape to the anonymity of the city.

Duncan drove his cas-chrom into the earth. It struck something hard and the shock jarred his arm and nipped the skin between his thumb and index finger. He watched the blister fill with blood. He scraped the earth away. It was a rock, possibly a boulder. It would take some moving. They would have to bring the horse up. Mist shrouded the Paps and he felt a coldness on his neck. He turned and saw the rain coming from the north.

The Text

Isobel stopped drying the teacup as she looked out of the kitchen window.

'They look funny. It doesn't seem right somehow.'

Kate, seated at the kitchen table, looked up from her laptop. Her mother's back framed the window.

'What seems funny?'

'The visitors.'

'Why are they funny?'

'They are all small. And they are Chinese.'

Kate joined her mother by the window. Four Chinese businessmen identically dressed in dark suits and blue anoraks were standing in the farmyard listening to John Ogilvie. The estate factor, dressed in a pin-striped suit and wellington boots, was talking to them, Kate assumed, about the farm. Her father was standing next to John Ogilvie. Kate smiled; he was playing with his tie.

'They are not that small. It's just that Dad and Mr. Ogilvie are tall.'

'I wonder why the Chinese are small?'

'They are not small, Mum. It's a myth.'

'It doesn't seem right.'

Isobel moved away from the window. She gave the teacup a last wipe and placed it on the tray.

'I mean, what do the Chinese know about farming on Jura?'

'Probably about as much as Mr. Van de Hoch. I don't think banking taught him anything about rearing livestock. Isn't that why they employ Dad?'

Isobel looked at cakes and scones piled up on the tray.

'Oh, it's so difficult. Do you think that they will like ginger cake and scones? I mean, they are Chinese.'

'Mum, they will love them. And if they don't, it won't stop them buying the place.'

'The Chinese owning the Ardross Estate.' Isobel shook her head. 'What are things coming to?'

Kate saved her work on the laptop and closed the lid.

'Mum, it's a company buying the estate. Chinese, Dutch or American – it makes no difference. The important thing is whether they will renovate the sheds and the milking parlour.'

'I will just set the table and leave them to it.'

Isobel picked up the tray of cakes and went into the living room.

Kate had put on her anorak.

'I'm off to see Ian, OK? I won't be back for dinner.'

'Don't be late.' Her mother's face appeared at the door. 'Tell Jane I will pop round this evening with the pattern she wanted.'

But her daughter had already left, and she watched her cross the now empty yard.

Isobel had dinner to prepare, Chinese or no Chinese. She picked up Kate's laptop and placed it on the dresser. Isobel looked at the computer, letting her fingers gently caress the shiny top. It was all so different now. Kate had taught her to text but she was always forgetting to turn her mobile on.

Kate would soon be off, the last one.

David an engineer on the rigs with his family in Aberdeen and Susan, married to Christopher, living down in the borders, every inch the farmer's wife. Now Kate. This time next year she would probably be at University. Probably!

Isobel sighed. There was no doubt Kate was intelligent and hard-working; whether Glasgow or Aberdeen was the only question. Aberdeen would be good. She could stay with David.

Isobel went to the old laundry to get the potatoes and carrots for dinner. She would miss Kate, more than the other two. Not only because she was the last, they were close, like best friends. They went shopping together and Isobel felt more comfortable in Kate's company than

with many of her Women's Rural friends. Susan had her
secrets and David had preferred his father's company,
until the awkward age of course, but Kate was open and
confident, easy in her own skin.

Isobel had just finished smoothing out the mashed
potatoes on the shepherd's pie when Douglas came in.
He pulled off his tie and dropped it on the table.
'That smells good.'
'How did it go?'
Douglas inspected the pie, his hand resting on his wife's
shoulder.
'They didn't say much. John seemed quite pleased.'
Douglas took off his tweed jacket.
'Don't know why I was there. Put me behind with the
milking. I'll go and get changed.'
'Did you say anything about the milking parlour?'
'John mentioned it. Oh yes, I think one of the heifers has
mastitis. I'll check her before milking. Is the Sinlox in
the fridge?'
'Should be.'
Isobel put the pie in the oven and went to get her jacket.

Milking over, Isobel mopped out the parlour while
Douglas took the cattle back to pasture. It was quiet, the
only sounds the slap of the mop and the pail scuffing
along the tiles. She stopped and, leaning on the mop,

gazed at the familiar sight. Of the twenty stalls only fifteen worked and keeping everything clean was strenuous work. If the new owners didn't invest it was just a matter of time before the parlour would have to be closed. The inspectors would see to that and they would be right; it wasn't fair on the cattle. Isobel and Douglas had visited David and Maire in Aberdeen last autumn, a chance to catch up and see the boys. They had broken their journey outside Aberfeldy, staying with Jim and Irene. They owned their own farm, two hundred head of dairy cattle. The milking parlour was new, state of the art, a circular design. That evening they had helped with the milking. It was so easy, and better for the cows. The milking finished, Douglas, Kate and Jim had stayed on in the parlour while Isobel helped Irene with the dinner. It was an enjoyable evening, with much laughter, but she had noticed how quiet Douglas had been the next day. She waited, and it came out once they had returned to Jura. A pump had jammed and Douglas cursed. Kate had looked at Isobel, her concern turning quickly into help, with a joke that caused her father to smile. Kate's kindness was effortless; it was who she was. Douglas had been like that once, before the responsibilities of the farm with an absentee landlord had started to overwhelm him.

Cleaning finished, Isobel closed the parlour door and made her solitary way to the chicken run with a bucket of grain. The children used to love this task. The chickens, so unthreatening, would follow the carefully-laid trail of grain into the chicken coop. David important and in charge, with Susan and little Kate following. They would return with their baskets of eggs. Kate would always put feather in her basket to make it 'look pretty'.

Isobel spooned the shepherd's pie onto the plate and handed it to Douglas. He added cabbage and a noisy squirt of HP sauce.
'She's off her milk as well.'
Isobel just added cabbage.
'Yes, I noticed that she was well down. Shall I phone the vet tomorrow?'
'No, I'll keep an eye on her. She's probably not worth the cost of a visit.'
They ate on in silence. Isobel could see that the visitors had disconcerted Douglas. They both knew that there had to be change, but the prospect was unsettling.
'Oh, yes. I almost forgot. Ian phoned. There are an extra three for the party for the clay pigeon shooting on Saturday. You might want to see if Stuart is available to help out.'
Douglas nodded.
'I'll check the targets. We should have plenty.'

The phone rang. It was Kate. She was staying over.

She could hear the gentle breathing of Douglas as she came up the stairs. Isobel looked at herself in the bathroom mirror and smiled sadly. What did she expect? She was fifty. Suddenly the two of them were getting old. Eight years ago she was barely out of her thirties and Kate was still in Primary School. And now...

She cleaned her teeth, washed her face and quietly made her way into the bedroom.

Kate turned on the hose to clean down the floor of the milking parlour and to encourage the cattle as they barged and stumbled their way into the yard. Isobel watched them come out. Accompanying the herd down the lane was a matter of habit; they could make their own way to pasture.

'Excuse me.'

Two walkers, dressed in their Rohan trousers and North Face anoraks were nervously watching the cows from the safety of the gate.

'Sorry to bother you.' They were English.

'Is it all right if we go through the yard? '

'Aye. It's part of the path. Shut the gate as you go'.

Isobel turned to go back into the parlour.

'We want to visit the deserted village.'

Once she had considered it pathetic, the need to explain themselves, as if to excuse their intrusion. But Kate had pulled her up short.

'They are only being polite.'

'You can't miss it.'

She did wonder, though, at the tourists' preoccupation with the tragic past. Things are always changing and it is never neat. She could see no benefit to be gained from dwelling on the injustices of one hundred and seventy years ago. There was more than enough to worry about in the present.

It looked like rain and so she grabbed her coat from the parlour while Kate opened the gate and the cattle lumbered through. The walkers were marching on ahead, free of the bovine threat.

It had been raining and Isobel noticed the ditches needed digging, but that wouldn't happen until the estate was sold. Mr Van de Hoch wasn't going to the expense of hiring a digger.

As the cows lumbered into the field Kate stood by the gate discouraging the more adventurous from continuing down the track. As they always did, mother and daughter leant on the gate as the cows browsed and wandered across the field. A shaft of sunlight fell on the Islay hills across the Sound.

'I think the rain will hold off.'

Isobel had wanted to say. 'We won't be doing this much longer with you off to Glasgow'. The acceptance letter had come through that morning. But it seemed ungracious, tinged with self-pity.

'We should go into Bowmore on Saturday. You will need to buy some things for college.'

Kate smiled.

'I am so excited. I really wanted Glasgow.' She stopped and Isobel wondered if Kate was on the verge of saying something that she thought disloyal. 'But I will miss all this.' Her enthusiasm seemed to evaporate. 'I hope I like the city. Anna gave up didn't she? Came back.'

Isobel put her arm around Kate. 'You'll be fine. It'll be great. David loved it. Come on. Things to do.'

They walked back to the farm. Isobel smiled ruefully; Anna came back because her father was drinking again and her mother needed help with the bairns. But there was no need for Kate to know that.

The shopping trip to Bowmore never happened. 'There will be more choice in Glasgow, Mum, and it will probably be cheaper.' The city was already staking its claim. They were standing on the quay at Port Askaig waiting for the ferry to Kennacraig and the mainland. Douglas had been very matter of fact at Kate's leaving and made a hasty exit with the dogs, to check on the sheep. Kate watched him until the jeep disappeared before bursting into tears. Isobel held her close and breathed in deeply to hold back her own.

Mary Girvan had come over with them on the short crossing from Feolin. She was on her way to Bowmore but was tarrying, taking the opportunity for a chat. She was concerned about old Mrs Daroch.

'I tell you, Isobel, it's not good. That cough has settled on her chest. The antibiotics can't seem to budge it. I go round all I can, but with winter coming... If you could look in occasionally.'

Isobel noticed that Kate had taken no part in the conversation but was impatiently looking down the Sound for the ferry. And for her part, Mary had noted Kate's leaving with a casual, 'Off to University. Oh, I heard that you were off. That's great,' before broaching her concern for Mrs Daroch.

They arrived in Glasgow just after midday. Isobel busied herself with carrying boxes from the car while Kate inspected her room and the hall of residence. On her third trip up the stairs Isobel saw Kate chatting to a tall dark-haired girl. Kate smiled.

'Oh, Julie, this is my Mum, Isobel.'

'Hello, Mrs. Drummond.'

Julie hesitated and then held out a tentative hand.

'Hello, Julie, nice to meet you. Have you just arrived as well?'

'No, Mrs Drummond. I came yesterday.' She turned to Kate. 'I'll pop round later.'

'Cool.'

Isobel smiled awkwardly. 'She seemed nice.'

Kate shrugged her shoulders. 'Have you seen my laptop?'

They went for a meal at an Italian restaurant. The conversation was tentative. Isobel wanted to talk about Kate's room and the hall of residence and what were her plans for the coming week, but for the first time in her life she felt uneasy in her daughter's company. This was Kate's world and inevitably Isobel would not be part of it. She would have to wait to be invited in. She didn't want to seem to be prying. Kate was preoccupied and Isobel felt she wanted to get back to the Hall of Residence in case she missed anything.

Isobel left early to drive back to Tarbet, 'before it gets dark'.

It was dusk when she arrived in Tarbet. She walked along the front and sat on a wall. The sun had disappeared behind the hills and there was a chill in the air. She phoned Douglas. Her reassurances about Kate and the hall of residence seemed facile. Douglas clambered onto the safe ground of affairs of the farm and the livestock. And then suddenly, as if an afterthought, 'Oh, yes. John

Ogilvie called. Apparently someone, from London I think, is up here. Wants to see the farm tomorrow.'

The ferry was early the following morning and in the room at the Failte Guest House Isobel made herself a cup of tea, carefully putting the teabag in the wastepaper bin. She preferred tea from the pot but this would have to do. She lay on the bed sipping her tea. She wondered what Kate was up to. She hoped that she would be back at the farm in time for the visitor. A cake was out of the question, but she could make scones. She suddenly felt tired and sad. She knew why, of course; she had been falling into these moods for a couple of years, but with the children, Kate, you made yourself get over it. She seemed to live in a continual state of flux, and she felt that she no longer had any control. She wasn't sure she could manage now with all the changes. She worried about Douglas. He had never been demonstrative, but when they were young and in love it didn't matter; it was who they were. But who were they now? With the children gone, she wasn't sure. For twenty five years they had been Mum and Dad, and now they would have to get to know each other again. She trusted Douglas; he was quiet and he was kind. But what would happen if whoever bought the estate didn't want Douglas? She put her teacup on the bedside table, the dark mood settled on her and in the sterile hotel room, with her head in her hands, Isobel quietly wept.

~ ~ ~ ~ ~ ~ ~ ~

Christmas Eve was shrouded by grey skies, as it usually was. The wind was down and it was mild; the ferry crossing for Susan and Christopher would be fine. They should arrive at Port Askaig just after three. Isobel looked at her watch; it was two thirty. She found the pastry- cutter in the drawer and started cutting out the fluted circles for the tin. Twelve would do. David and Maire were having Christmas at home with the boys. They wouldn't visit until New Year's Eve. Susan and Christopher's farm was arable, and his brother could take care of the few livestock they had. It was good they could get away occasionally; things would be different when kids arrived. Isobel had just placed the pastry circles in the tin when she heard Kate laughing in the yard. Isobel looked up. Kate had changed. Not only the new haircut and highlights; there was something more defined about her. Only three months, but the softness of the schoolgirl had gone; there was an independence and a certainty about her. She had become her own woman in a way Isobel felt that she never had. Then there was Georgi, the Bulgarian boyfriend.

'He's not really a boyfriend, Mum. It's not like that.'

The photograph on the iPhone suggested otherwise, and without a doubt he was handsome. Studying for an MBA in Glasgow. *Why not Sofia?* she wondered, but it was all change nowadays.

Kate came into the kitchen.

'The new parlour's incredible, Mum.'

Isobel smiled.

'Yes, isn't it? Makes you wonder how we managed before.'

'Dad says it was put up in a month.'

Isobel started spooning the mincemeat into the pastry.

'Yes, we were lucky. We had a good spell in October.'

'That smells good.' A finger darted into the bowl. Not quite so grown-up, maybe.

'That's enough of that, Missy.'

'So this Mr. Fletcher seems alright?'

'I've only met him once. Seems nice. He's renovating the main house.'

'Canadian.'

'Yes. His father has a cattle farm in Saskatchewan.'

'So he understands cattle?'

Isobel put the mince pies into the oven and wiped her hands on her apron.

'I suppose so. He noticed the drainage needed doing. His great grandfather was born in Scotland, moved to Canada in the thirties. You will meet him. He's having a

New Years' party. It seems the whole island is invited. Fond of his kilt apparently.'

The phone rang and Kate answered it.

'It's Mary Girvan.'

'Oh, that will be about the funeral. Make us a cup of tea, love.'

Isobel sipped her tea.

'Will you come to the funeral?'

'Of course.'

'You know she was Brown Owl when I was in the Brownies. She was kind. You didn't have to try too hard to get your badges.'

Isobel smiled at the memory of Mrs Daroch.

Kate took a biscuit. 'Do you think Mr. Fletcher is serious?'

'Who knows? He seems to have lots of money. Hedge funds, or something like that.'

'Hmm.'

Kate drained her cup and placed it on the sideboard. A car drew up in the yard.

'It's Susan and Christopher.'

Kate ran out.

Isobel went to the kitchen door. Kate was hugging Susan while Christopher was taking the bags out of the car. Two confident young women. Isobel smiled; she felt proud.

Susan came up the path and when she reached her mother she hugged her. Isobel noticed she was tearful.
'Mum, I'm pregnant.'

~ ~ ~ ~ ~ ~ ~ ~

Isobel took the mobile from the charger and put it in her pocket. Susan was due and Isobel didn't want to miss an important text. She had been texting Susan every day. Mary Girvan had made a joke about Isobel being on Facebook next. She turned off the radio, put on her boots and went into the yard. On the *Today Programme* was news of the collapse of Strathmore Holdings. Douglas had shaken his head.
'I think that's Fletcher's lot.'
It was too early to phone John Ogilvie at the Estate Office.
Douglas put on his jacket.
'I've got to rush.'
He stopped by the door; he looked worried.
'John was talking to the accountants the other day. He mentioned they were concerned. Something about financial irregularities. I didn't take it in. You've got John's mobile number. Text him and ask him if there's anything to worry about. Get him to phone me. He's got my mobile.'

Douglas had driven off to help supervise the drainage work.

Although it was only 7.30 the sun was high in a cloudless June sky. The air was crisp and fresh. It was strange to think of Kate this summer, working at a pop up café in Glasgow, saving for the trip to Sofia.

As she walked across the yard Isobel sent the text. In the milking parlour she started to hose down the milking stalls still gleaming, nine months since the wary cows first entered, urged on by Douglas. She was going to the cupboard for the disinfectant when her mobile beeped.

It was a text.

The Twenty

Keith opened his wallet, a single twenty pound note.
Enough for a pint, but a round would leave him short.
'Same again Donald.'
Donald, ever correct, took a fresh glass and placed it
under the tap.
'So, off tomorrow, Keith.'
Keith smiled and nodded.
'One thirty.'
Donald placed the glass on the beer mat in front of
Keith. Keith offered the twenty pound note. Donald
waved it away.
'This is on the house.'
'Thank you, old chap.'
Keith smiled and raised his glass to Donald. He took a
small sip; he would have to make this last. Duncan and
Ian were early evening drinkers and would be off to their
dinner soon – save the embarrassment of being seen to
not buy a round.
'So this is really it. Off to pastures new, eh Keith?'

Duncan wasn't fishing. He was being kind. Everyone knew.

'Yes. Quite a change.'

'Bolton is it?' Ian this time.

'No, it's Bradford, isn't it, Keith?'

'That's right Duncan. With my brother. Just a few weeks while I get settled.'

The conversation died. Donald took to wiping glasses.

'Trouble with a fuel injector.'

'That's not good.'

'It's leaking. Fumes in the car.'

Ian and Duncan fell to discussing Ian's ageing Berlingo and the virtues of replacement models. Keith was thankful. Their interest was polite, but they weren't friends. Not really friends. That was the problem. He didn't have any friends on the Island. Janet had made friends. She was good at that. The church was full at her funeral; all who could come had come. People had been kind. Well, they were kind, but Keith found it hard being an object of pity. He had cut them out, not rudely, just kept himself to himself, the odd pint at the hotel in the early evening. He took another sip of beer.

Keith felt a hand on his shoulder.

'All the best, Keith, if I don't see you tomorrow.'

Ian held out his hand.

'We're going to miss you. Place won't be the same without you on the end of the bar.'

Keith smiled.

Duncan joined him.

'You take care big man. Let us know how you are getting on.'

Hands were shaken and the pair took their leave with a wave.

Donald pushed a double whiskey towards Keith and indicated the parting friends, then went to a table in the bar and started checking invoices against his records, leaving Keith alone. He's a good barman Keith thought – sensitive to customers' feelings.

Keith poured the baked beans into the pan and turned the plate on. He put two slices of bread in the toaster. He had run out of butter but it didn't matter. He would have something to eat on the ferry tomorrow. He still had the twenty.

The kitchen was bare. They had taken everything. The coldness, the bitterness, it had been cruel. Janet would have been horrified to see her sons acting like that. But they had never liked him. Toby, the eldest, had made that plain from the off. And Justin, well Justin followed Toby. Once the house was sold they came and cleared everything out into a van, and off the island. It was all Keith could do to stop them filching his few possessions.

They had stayed at the Hotel and he knew that they had spread their poison, portraying him as a leech and a loser, a gin-soaked con-man who had wormed his way into Janet's affections when she was vulnerable after the divorce. What did they know? It was Janet who had made the running, looking for companionship after that brute Gerald. Toby was certainly a chip off the old block. Janet had sworn him to secrecy and Keith had respected that. 'He's their father, after all'. At that time he had the money, the inheritance. Janet had to wait for the divorce settlement and Gerald fought it every inch of the way. They had never talked of marriage, it didn't seem appropriate.

Keith took the plate to the sink, washed and dried it and carefully placed it in the cupboard. He wouldn't leave a mess. They had left a mattress with blankets and a light. It was only eight but Keith got ready for bed – long day tomorrow. He decided to read; they had taken the TV and radio.

They had had fun, the trips and the cruises. Keith wondered now whether the inheritance hadn't thrown him a bit off kilter. Giving up the job, playing the stock exchange, it all seemed so easy, better than store manager at Argos. He had been the life and soul of the party, until he lost the lot. Not really his fault; no-one saw it coming.

It shook his confidence. Well, it would, wouldn't it. One moment at the top of the tree with no worries, the next... Keith opened the book. *Sharpe's Company*. He'd read it before but couldn't remember what happened.

The island had been Janet's idea. The quiet life. She had loved it, jam-making and quilting, lots of friends. Five years, good years. Money had been tight but they had got by, courtesy of the divorce. 'Well, Gerald had to be good for something'. Keith had settled in to the routine but he always felt beholden. It was his fault, he didn't have to feel that way. Janet didn't see it like that, but he wondered what people thought and he couldn't help it, he felt useless. After all, he wasn't a fisherman or a crofter, and he certainly couldn't paint pictures for the tourists.

And then the stroke. Keith put the book down. That morning they had been laughing about *Strictly Come Dancing*. Nothing strange in that, they often laughed. But she was happy, really happy and it had made Keith feel good. Back from his early evening pint and there she was, on the kitchen floor. He lay back on the mattress. Nothing made sense, and the stillness of grief left him empty and without purpose.

Keith, his case packed, stood on the concrete jetty and watched as the ferry made its way towards the island. It was overcast and still, and the ferry was on time. He saw Donald, papers in hand, talking to the harbour master and they disappeared into his office. Keith didn't like goodbyes, at least not like this, and was pleased there was no one to see him off.

It was good of Roger to put him up, Keith could tell he wasn't keen. God knows what he was going to do. Fifty nine, no chance of a job and a few years before the pension. He looked over at the Paps of Jura, the tops in cloud. He wouldn't be back this way again.

The ferry docked and Keith made his way down the slipway.

CPSIA information can be obtained
at www.ICGtesting.com
Printed in the USA
LVHW010351161221
706369LV00011B/915